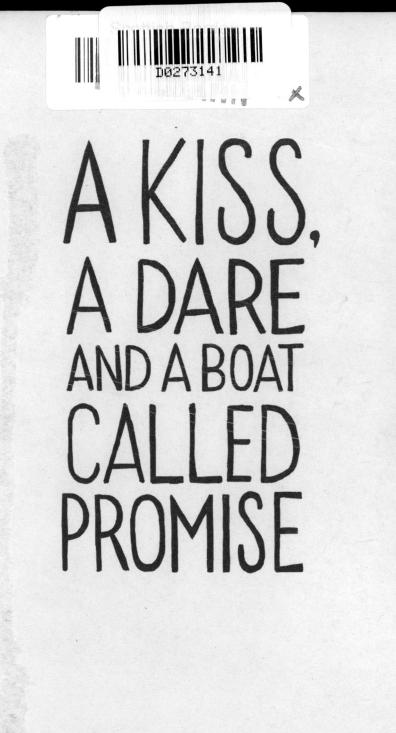

A KISS,
A DARE
AND A BOAT
CALLED
PROMISE

About the Author

Fiona Foden grew up in a tiny Yorkshire village called Goose Eye. At seventeen she landed her dream job on a teenage magazine in Scotland, and went on to be editor of *Bliss, More!* and *Just Seventeen* magazines. She now lives in Lanarkshire, Scotland with her husband Jimmy and their children Sam, Dexter and Erin.

When she's not writing, Fiona likes to play her sax and flute and go out running with her mad rescue dog Jack. *A Kiss, a Dare and a Boat Called Promise* is her third book for teenagers.

Also by Fiona Foden

Life, Death and Gold Leather Trousers
Cassie's Crush

A KISS, A DARE AND A BOAT CALLED PROMISE

FIONA FODEN

SCHOLASTIC

First published in the UK in 2013 by Scholastic Children's Books
An imprint of Scholastic Ltd
Euston House, 24 Eversholt Street
London, NW1 1DB, UK
Registered office: Westfield Road, Southam, Warwickshire, CV47 0RA
SCHOLASTIC and associated logos are trademarks and/or
registered trademarks of Scholastic Inc.

ISBN 978 1407 13685 1

A CIP catalogue record for this book is available
from the British Library.

Printed and bound by CPI Group (UK) Ltd, Croydon, CR0 4YY
Papers used by Scholastic Children's Books are made
from wood grown in sustainable forests.

1 3 5 7 9 10 8 6 4 2

www.scholastic.co.uk/zone

For Lily D with love

DO YOU BELIEVE IN LUCK?

I do — sort of. Maybe it's because I live on a boat instead of in a house or flat. Boaters can be pretty superstitious — at least, the ones I know are.

I don't mean we concoct spells or have black cats prowling about on our boats. We're just normal people who happen to live on water instead of land. But there's one thing a boater would never do, and that's change the name of their boat. It's meant to bring bad luck. Ours is called Promise and, even if I woke up one morning with a wild urge to paint it over and change it to, I don't know — "Primrose", just for a joke — I wouldn't actually dare. When your boat is also your home, you don't want to risk anything bad happening, do you?

But I believe in good luck too. Here's a secret: I have a lucky tin. It's old and scruffy with "Swallow's Toffees" in gold lettering on its spotty blue lid. But it's not the tin that's important. It's the stuff inside.

*There are drawings, notes and newspaper cuttings –
things that belonged to my dad. When he died, Mum
was so upset, she wanted to get rid of all of his things.
She said she couldn't bear to see them any more.
Everything made her cry back then, and I didn't
want to make things worse. I did want some of Dad's
things, though, and I started to come across bits and
pieces at the bottom of drawers, or slipped in-between
the pages of books, almost as if they were waiting for
me to find them. Without saying a word to Mum, or
to my big brother Ryan, I secretly gathered everything
up until the toffee tin was nearly full. I thought of it
as my lucky tin, and as the months passed, life became
brighter again, as if Dad was somehow looking after
us. The other boaters rallied round to help us and a
local hotel took Mum on as a chef. Then, best of all,
a pea-green boat called Tarragon chugged down the
river and moored next to us. It belonged to a cheerful
couple who had a daughter called Bella. We became
best friends straight away. I found a silver ring nestling
in the grass on the riverbank, as if a magpie had dropped
it, and I gave it to Bella so she has her own lucky
thing too.*

*It's five years since Dad died, and Bella is still the
only person who knows about my tin. I have my own
cabin to sleep in, and under my bed there's a loose
bit of wood with a space underneath. That's where I
keep it, away from prying eyes. Most of the time Dad*

seems blurry in my mind, like a faded photo. But occasionally, when I get out my tin, he's not blurry at all.

Then he's absolutely real.

Sometimes, weeks go by and I don't even look in the tin. But I always know it's there.

CHAPTER One

At last, it's here. The final day of term and the *real* start of summer. Just a few hours to scramble through – we finish school early today – then freedom, for weeks on end.

Morning light is filtering through the thin curtain at my cabin window. I can hear Mum pottering about, and there's a slight rocking as another boat chugs by. Normally, I don't notice the gentle swaying from side to side. You don't when you live on water. When friends who have houses come to visit, they go, "Whoa!" and stagger about, throwing out their arms and acting all wobbly, as if we're on a stormy sea instead of a quiet stretch of river which hardly ripples at all.

Today, though, I *do* notice the rocking. I lie in my narrow wooden bed, as still as anything, until the sound of the passing engine dies away and it's just Mum, chopping something in the kitchen.

"Josie!" she calls out. "Come on – get up. You don't want to be late for school on the last day."

Actually, I *do* want. What's the point of the last day anyway? No one does any work…

"Josie, it's nearly eight o'clock!"

OK, OK. But what about my hairy big brother? Isn't it *his* last day too? I know he's not out of bed either, because faint music is coming from his cabin.

"And Ryan," Mum barks, "if you don't get up now, you'll be going to school in your pyjamas."

She doesn't mean that. Since he turned sixteen, Ryan has stopped wearing pyjamas to bed. Apparently, they are "immature". After being intensely body-shy pretty much all of his life, he has also developed a habit of wandering about in his saggy old *South Park* boxers – even up on the deck, i.e., in public. Oh, and Promise has suddenly become "far too cramped", he reckons. It is pretty small, but living here still suits me just fine (this might have something to do with the fact that I'm one of the shortest girls in year eight). Anyway, it's hardly Promise's fault that Ryan has sprouted from being a normal-sized boy to a great gangly giraffe of nearly six feet.

I'm out of bed now, still in my "babyish" PJs (*South Park* pants are *deeply* mature, obviously), shouting "Coming!" to Mum. Then it's straight into my normal getting-ready-for-school routine: white shirt on, plus black trousers, socks and black canvas lace-ups (not the most stylish of footwear, admittedly, but best for cycling to school). I peer into the mirror on my cabin wall –

a few years ago I decorated it with glittery butterfly stickers, which I realize are *far* too girly for a thirteen-year-old – and tie back my long dark hair. It has a mind of its own if I leave it loose. I also remind myself that one day, I might actually be tall enough to see my reflection in the mirror without having to stand on tiptoe. What was Mum thinking, putting it up so high? Perhaps she thought it'd encourage me to grow faster – e.g., eat more vegetables, ha ha.

"Ooh, you've made strawberry tarts," I exclaim. "They look fantastic, Mum." I'm in the kitchen now – our kitchen *area*, I mean, which is actually the far end of our living room, next to the five worn, wooden steps that take you up on to the deck. Towards the bow of the boat – the front end – are our three separate cabins, and the loo and shower room, which is so tiny that Ryan can hardly fit into it any more.

"Thanks." Mum grins, her blue eyes glinting as she pushes back her wavy fair hair. "So they should. I was up at six this morning getting the pastry started."

Murphy, our wiry light-brown terrier, jumps out of his basket and nuzzles his head against my legs. I give him a hug and tickle, then go to grab a tart from the tray. "Hey, get your hands off, greedy." Mum gently slaps my hand away. "Have cereal or something. These are meant to be for later."

"Go on, just one. I need to keep up my strength if I'm going to learn anything today. . ." Before she can say anything else, I'm cramming the sweet, fruity tart into my mouth, which, like some magical, strawberry-scented magnet, has the effect of drawing Ryan out of his cabin.

"Tarts, great," he mumbles, stuffing his face and squinting in the morning light, like a bear emerging from hibernation.

"There'll be none left for the party at this rate," Mum says, although we know she doesn't mean it. As soon as Ryan and I are out of her hair, she'll be rolling and cutting and baking loads more, the aroma of pastry wafting down the river in a sugary blur. By the time we're home, Promise will no longer be just an old wooden boat, and home to three people plus a scruffy dog, but a luscious-smelling, floating patisserie.

I love the French name for cake shop. It's so much more mouth-watering than plain old "bakery", and you'd be amazed at the deliciousness that can come out of a tiny ancient oven on an even more ancient boat. Mum is a magical baker – she works part-time in a nearby country hotel where posh ladies meet for cream teas. Today, though, she's staying here on Promise, getting the food ready and putting up the decorations. We have a party every year – not just my family but all the boaters who live here – on the day school breaks up for summer. That's what it's like on the river – parties, celebrations, all of us kind of living together but having our own space, too. We're constantly in and out of each other's boats, and I spend as much time on Bella's next door as I do on Promise.

"Josie? You ready?" Bella is on our deck now, peeping down through the hatch, her short blonde plaits sticking out from beneath her cycle helmet.

"Yeah, coming," I call back. There's just time to give Murphy another belly tickle and Mum a quick hug. She doesn't see me secretly cupping my hand around a tart for Bella. Ryan barges past me and hurries up to the deck, tearing off on his bike before Bella and I have even unfastened ours from the tree they're padlocked to. These days, he'd rather *die* than be spotted cycling to school with me.

I clip on my helmet and we set off, past the row of boats which are moored along our sleepy stretch of river, where I've lived my whole life. All the boats here are people's homes, and we're *all* friends – in some ways, we're like one big family, which is great for me as I don't have much family of my own. "Wish we could fast-forward the next five hours," I tell Bella as we speed along the path.

"Me too," she agrees, her mouth still full of Mum's tart.

"D'you think many people will come this year?"

"Oh yeah!" she exclaims. "Our parties are famous, aren't they?" She's right; after all, you don't often see twelve boats all lit up with lanterns and people dancing on their decks. It was Bella's mum's idea to start having a huge party to celebrate the start of the summer holidays. Soon, all the boaters were joining in, even though most of them don't have kids. Apart from Christmas, when there are yet more celebrations, it's the highlight of our year.

Filled with excitement now, we turn on to the tree-lined lane which leads to the village a couple of miles away. That's where our school is. As five of us boaters go there (me and Bella, obviously, plus Ryan and his mates Tyler and Jake) there's none of that, "Ew, you live on a boat, you're a stinky water gypsy" stuff we hear about. Everyone's used to the way we live. They don't make a big deal out of it. In fact, I suspect some of them are even a tiny bit jealous that their homes can't go anywhere.

Bella and I start racing each other along the flat country lanes, and we're actually on time for once (see, Mum? Not late on the precious last day after all).

And somehow, the next five hours fly by until, in what feels like a blink, we're cycling back home again towards the river.

"It looks amazing!" I yell as the boats come into view. We can already see brightly coloured bunting strung between trees along the riverbank, and the sound of chatter and laughter drifts over the water towards us. There's been more baking going on, too, the delicious smells making us cycle as fast as we can. Bella and I are laughing as we throw down our bikes and jump on to my boat.

People are already gathering on the decks, which are all decorated with buckets of flowers and those little plastic windmills that spin around in the breeze. Music is playing, and our mums stop setting out plates of freshly made brownies on Tarragon's deck and beckon us over to try them. Bella's dad, Charlie, hands us cups of home-made lemonade, which we carry from boat to boat as we dart around, saying hi to everyone. People are playing guitars, tin whistles, bongos and flutes. Even Ryan, who's officially far too old to be excited about anything our mums have organized, has grabbed a guitar and is joining in.

I turn to Bella and smile. "Just think, we're free for six and a half weeks."

"*And* you're staying with us tomorrow night," she adds, reminding me that Mum is taking Promise up the river to the boatyard tomorrow, where she's booked in for repairs (that's Promise, not Mum, that's being fixed, by the way. A boat is always a "she" – I don't know why but it feels right). It looks like there's a small leak under our floor, as it's a bit damp down there. We're all praying it'll be a cheap, simple job to fix it.

"Yeah," I say. "Just two nights, Mum reckons. She's hoping to pick up Promise on Saturday."

"The longer the better," Bella says with a grin. "I love it when you stay with us."

Then there's no time to discuss it because Mum is asking me to fetch more drinks from our fridge, and Bella's told to hand out plates of pastries. Soon jam-jar lanterns are lit, and the warm July evening is beautiful with flickering lights reflecting off the river. The party has spread along the line of boats to the huge red one at the end, where Ryan's mates Tyler and Jake live. Even the oldies are joining in, like Maggie and Phil, whose scruffy old barge Mucky Duck attracts any stray cat looking for cosy spot by their stove. When Ryan, Tyler and Jake carry guitars and drums on to the riverbank for an impromptu performance, everyone gathers around and cheers. The sky darkens, and some of the adults are definitely tipsy by now. Everyone just laughs and cheers when, for a dare, Tyler strips down to his boxers and plunges into the river.

"What a party," Mum says later, grabbing my hand.

"The best ever," I agree, hugging her. Although she's smiling, her eyes are gleaming wet in the moonlight, and I know she's thinking, *Your dad would have loved this.* I know he would, too. Then Bella yells for me to join her on her deck, where music is being cranked up again, and people I don't even know, who the other boaters have invited, are all dancing and asking, "So when's the next one?"

It's nearly two in the morning when the party finally fades and I crawl into bed. Although I'm exhausted, it's impossible to drift off to sleep, so I get up and reach for the loose bit of wood under my bed. I lift it away and fumble for the tin.

Back in bed, I prise off the lid and take out the book of drawings Dad made when he was little. There are only eight pages, frayed at their edges and held together with a rusty staple. On the cover he's written "The Seven Wonders of the Ancient World". Then on each page he's drawn – in pencil, so it's pretty faded – these amazing places like the Egyptian pyramids and the Hanging Gardens of Babylon. And at the bottom of the back page he's written his name, *Davy Lennox, age nine*. I love imagining him sitting there, drawing this book, the way I spent hours with pens and paper when I was younger, because we've never had a TV on Promise.

Like I said, I don't often feel sad that Dad's not here. Because if I want to feel close to him I just look at his Wonders of the Ancient World book, and all the photos and yellowy newspaper cuttings about him winning various cross-country races. In one photo he's on a track, in a vest and shorts, his dark hair flying and a look of pure joy on his face.

He was a runner, my dad, and an artist too. And he's as real to me as Charlie, Bella's dad, is to her.

I slip out of bed, put the tin in its hiding place and snuggle back under my covers. Charlie is still strumming his guitar on Tarragon's deck, and Bella's mum, Kate, is singing. As my mum joins in, a single thought fills my head:

Today was perfect. This is going to be the best summer ever. . .

That feeling's still there as I open my eyes, and the squawk of a duck tells me that morning has come.

CHAPTER

Two

I'm bleary as anything as I get dressed in jeans and a stripy T-shirt. "Josie! Ryan! Come on, lazybones," Mum calls out. "I need some help to clear this place up. I told the boatyard guy that Promise will be with him by lunchtime so we really need to get a move on. . ." I emerge from my cabin, yawning loudly. "Are you sure you're happy to stay behind and hang out with Bella today?" Mum asks. "We'll be back by early evening."

"Yeah, of course," I reply.

"Can't we set off later?" Ryan has appeared from his cabin. "It's the holidays, Mum. I need a lie-in. . ."

"Let's just get this place sorted," she says, shooing Murphy away from a spillage of crisps on the floor.

"Do I *have* to come with you?" Ryan groans.

"Yes, you do," Mum retorts. "I need your help. Remember, it's a lot further than Frank's yard." Frank owned the nearest boatyard to us; it was where we always took Promise for repairs. He used to give me and Ryan lollies you could use as whistles, and we'd be allowed to clamber all over the boats which had been lifted out of the river by the huge, rusty crane.

He's retired now and shut down his yard. Promise is booked in at a new place but, even though it *is* miles further away, Mum doesn't really need any help to get there. She can handle our boat perfectly well by herself. She just wants company, that's all. "We'll make a day of it," she's telling my brother, while I gather up jam jars with burnt-out candles inside. "We can explore the town and get fish and chips. Charlie's kindly offered to come and pick us up around teatime when he's finished at work."

"*Why* would I want to do that?" Ryan is talking as if she's suggested a trip to the dentist's.

"Because ... I thought it'd be nice for us to do something together." Mum sounds hurt, and I wish he'd stop being so snarly.

"Hmm." He snorts. "Great start to the summer."

She turns, anger flashing in her eyes now. "Stop moaning, Ryan. I'm worried enough about how I'm going to pay for this work. Hopefully just a couple of planks will need replacing and it won't be too expensive."

"Maybe the boatyard man will wait a few weeks for his money," I suggest.

"Why would he do that, Josie?" she snaps.

Whoa ... *OK*. "I just thought he might, if you explained."

"Explained what, exactly?"

Oh no. After all the excitement of the party, Mum's come back down to earth with a bump. I can tell she's worried and stressed. "That we might not be able to pay it all at once," I murmur.

Ryan sighs loudly, and Mum's face softens as she says, "This isn't Frank, Josie. The guy sounded pretty grumpy on the phone, actually. We'll just have to hope for the best, all right? The leak doesn't seem that bad. Hopefully it's nothing too serious." She musters a brave smile.

I glance at my brother, then at Mum, and before I can stop myself, I'm saying, "*I'll* come if you like, Mum. Ryan doesn't have to."

"Yesss!" Ryan exclaims, punching the air. "Thanks, sis."

Mum gives me a quizzical look. "You sure, Josie? I thought you and Bella had plans for today. . ."

I shrug. "Only swimming at the lake, and we've got all summer for that."

"Well," she says, smiling, "I suppose it'll be nicer to have someone with me who actually wants to be there, rather than acting as if they're about to have their teeth pulled out."

This makes me sound so helpful and generous, doesn't it? And I am – some of the time. But the truth is, because the other boaters are always popping in for chats, Mum and I hardly ever have any time together.

Very occasionally, I wonder what it would be like to have a teeny bit more privacy, so it's just us.

Twenty minutes later, Ryan's got dressed and wandered off with Murphy to Jake and Tyler's boat, and I've told a slightly disappointed Bella that I won't be around today after all. She wishes us luck and waves us goodbye – and we're off.

That sounds like we *zoom* down the river, hair flying behind us, but in fact someone with a bad limp could keep up with us. Murphy could outpace Promise, and he's ten, eleven or even older (he was a stray – we got him from Dogs Trust – so no one knows his actual age). It's more of a steady amble along the curve of the river, with dense woods, then gently sloping fields, on both sides.

The occasional boat passes us, and the people on them give us a smile and a nod hello. The sun warms our faces as we chug along, not talking much, just enjoying the peace. We pass Frank's old boatyard, the rickety shed all boarded up and looking as if it could blow down in a breeze. And finally, we start to see houses as the river takes us into a small town. We've almost come out of the other side of it when Mum spots a sign which says "McIntyre Boat Repair & Maintenance". "That's the place," she says, slowing down the engine for the last few metres, then expertly guiding Promise alongside the wooden quay.

We're tying her up when a man approaches us. "Hi there," Mum says, smiling. "I'm looking for Bill, he's expecting us. . ."

"Yup, that's me." He's wearing dark blue overalls smeared with oil and paint, and has a bushy grey moustache that doesn't match the raven black of his hair. "Blimey," he adds with a chuckle, "it's a wonder you got here in that old thing."

Mum frowns as she steps on to the bank. "Her engine's fine. We have it serviced every year—"

"I'm not talking about her engine." He laughs again, giving Promise's gleaming wooden side a firm slap and looking her up and down as if he's never seen such a sorry excuse for a boat in his life. Frank was never like this. He always praised us for taking such good care of Promise, and said he looked forward to working on her, that it was more like a hobby for him when an antique boat like ours came along. "How old is she anyway?" Bill asks abruptly.

"Over eighty years," Mum says as we follow him into an ugly concrete building. Greasy propellers, engine parts and pots of paint are strewn about on the dirty floor. The place is a mess. I can't imagine Bill managing to fix anything properly, let alone our precious boat. Surely we could have found someone better than him to do the job?

Still muttering about the state of our beloved home, he opens the door to a flimsy-looking glass-walled office in the far corner of the building. Taking a seat at the desk, he motions for Mum to sit opposite him. As there are no other chairs, I lurk in the corner, hoping we can get this over and done with as quickly as possible. "So . . . you think there's a problem with the hull?" he begins.

Sounding irritated now, Mum tells him about the small leak in the bilges – that's the part underneath the floor. My gaze skims the dirty mugs littering his desk, and the old computer in the corner, covered in grubby fingerprints and splashes of what looks like coffee. "I've always looked after her," Mum goes on, "so it shouldn't be anything too serious. The whole hull was checked last summer, by Frank Jackson." *That's right – Frank, who didn't keep giving us sneery looks. . .*

Bill grunts, and I notice wiry grey hairs poking out of his nose. "Just out of interest," he says, "I don't suppose you know who built her?"

"It was my granddad," Mum says with a trace of pride, "when he was only eighteen years old."

Bill snorts as if to say, *That figures.*

"He designed her himself," she goes on, "and she was such a success that a company started building boats from his original design, all by hand. There used to be hundreds but as far as I know, Promise is the only one left."

"Hmmm," Bill says. "I could tell she was someone's wacky project."

I glare at him. How dare he talk about my great-granddad like that? He did something amazing, and was pretty famous, at least among people who care about boats. What's with the "wacky project" stuff?

Mum is fizzing mad now – I can almost smell it radiating off her – and she clamps her mouth shut as he makes some notes in a grubby pad. "I'll have her out of the water by mid-afternoon," he tells her. "Phone me at the end of the day and we'll see what the damage is."

"OK," Mum says, pushing back her chair with a scrape as she gets up. Although I'm not keen on leaving Promise with this horrible man, it's a relief to escape from his stale, smoky office and step back out into the blue-skied afternoon.

"It doesn't matter if we like him or not," Mum says as we leave the mess of the boatyard behind and start to head into town. "I just hope we can trust him to do a good job."

"Hmm," I mumble.

She turns to me and smiles. "Come on, cheer up. Let's have a look around, make the most of the day. We've got a few hours before Charlie's coming to pick us up."

"OK, Mum," I say with a loud sigh. I try to enjoy our afternoon, I really do. Yet, as we peer into the horribly expensive gift shops on the high street, I start to wish Ryan had come instead, and that Bella and I were splashing about in the lake, then drying off and hanging out in the dappled sunshine at the edge of the forest. Mum spots a museum in an old church, and we decide to go in, but the only interesting thing is a beehive which is half inside, half outside the building. On the inside, you can watch the bees all skittering about under a sheet of glass. They remind me of how I feel when strangers wander along the riverbank and stop to peer in through our windows. One morning, I woke up in my cabin to see a man's big pink face gawping in at me. I screamed in shock and shouted for Mum. "I didn't realize anyone lived here," the man called back, mortified, as Mum ran out to see what was going on.

After the thrilling museum, we have a picnic of baguettes and Cokes in a park where all the flowers are planted in neat rows. As a faint summer shower starts to fall, we shelter under a huge tree, where Mum pulls her mobile from her pocket.

"Hello, Bill?" she says to the boatyard man. "It's Helen Lennox. I wondered if you'd managed to have a look at Promise yet." She pauses, and I see her mouth setting into a frown. She's nodding and saying, "Right ... right..."

And it's obvious that something is *not* right at all.

CHAPTER
Three

"What is it?" I hiss at Mum.

Still clutching her phone, she waves me away as if I'm a buzzing insect. I know I'm small for my age but – *hello?* She's carrying on her conversation as if I'm not even here.

"What's wrong?" I mouth at her. "What is it, Mum?"

She shakes her head and turns her back to me. "I . . . I had no idea," she goes on. "As I said, Frank Jackson had her out of the water last year and he never mentioned anything about rotten timbers. . ." My stomach feels as heavy as the dark clouds above. Rotten timbers? What are they *talking* about? "Fine," Mum says quickly. "Look, my daughter and I are standing out in the rain here. We'll come over as soon as we can." She finishes the call, rams her mobile back into the pocket of her old, faded jeans and snatches my hand as if I'm a little kid.

There's a cafe at the far end of the park, made of glass

like a pointy-roofed greenhouse. Still holding my hand tightly, Mum barges straight in and stomps towards a table for two. "What did he say?" I ask, perching on the seat opposite her.

She bites her lip. "Seems that Promise hasn't exactly lived up to her name, Josie."

"What did he say about rotten timbers?" I ask as the smiling waitress comes over to our table.

"What would you like?" she asks.

"Er . . . I'll have tea," Mum mutters. "Hot chocolate for you, Josie?"

"Yes, please." The sense that something bad is happening has left me feeling chilled.

"Mum," I start as the waitress returns to the counter, "*please* tell me what's happening."

"Just give me a moment to think, Josie." We sit in bleak silence, and I have to bite my lip to stop myself from bombarding her with more questions. Mum nods her thanks as our drinks arrive, and as she stirs her tea, her forehead crinkles with worry.

"Well, I assume it's not good news," I mutter finally, spooning froth off the top of my hot chocolate.

Mum clears her throat. "I'm sorry, Josie. It's just come as a horrible shock. He says virtually the whole hull is rotten, can you believe it? Reckons she's a write-off. I can't understand it."

"He's talking rubbish," I exclaim. The hull's the whole underneath of the boat. I mean practically *all* of it. "She'd sink if it was," I add, deciding I was right about Bill being a complete idiot.

"Well, that's what he told me," Mum says firmly. "Reckons the wood's like a sponge — you could poke your finger through it, he said. I can't believe I didn't know."

"Can't he just replace the worst planks?"

Mum shakes her head. "He seems to think not."

"Why not? Is it because of money? We could save up, find something to sell—"

"He said it's not a matter of a few planks, Josie. It's the whole boat. We'll have to get back over there and see for ourselves, OK? I just hope he's got it wrong. Then we can take her to another boatyard to have the work done. . ." Mum looks as if she might cry now, but is holding it together for my sake. "I don't know, though," she adds in a shaky voice. "Maybe she can't be fixed. I mean, I don't have my granddad's original plans for Promise, and people just don't make boats like that any more."

"We can't just give up on her," I say firmly.

"No, I'm not suggesting we do. But I think we should be prepared for the worst. . ."

I jump up from my seat. "Come on, Mum. Let's go and find out for ourselves." I stomp towards the door with Mum hurrying behind me.

"Excuse me!" The waitress charges after us as we step outside. "You haven't paid."

"Oh, I'm so sorry," Mum says, blushing as she digs into her scruffy brown shoulder bag for her purse. She hands the woman some coins.

"That's OK," the waitress says with a tight smile.

My cheeks are burning too as we stand outside the cafe. "You'd never give up on Murphy like that," I mumble.

"What are you talking about, Josie?"

"When something's wrong with Murphy, we still get him medicine or whatever he needs. You'd never say 'we should be prepared for the worst' with him, like there's no hope."

Mum frowns at me. "I'm just trying to be realistic, sweetheart. Bill said Promise has had it, all right? And although I didn't like the man, I can't see any reason for him to lie to us."

"But Murphy's old," I argue, "and things go wrong with him sometimes. . ."

Mum shakes her head. "He's a dog, Josie! A living thing. That's completely different."

Is it, though? As we head back towards the boatyard, I find myself wishing there was such a thing as a vet for boats.

As soon as we arrive back at the yard, Bill starts prodding at Promise's hull. "Look at these timbers," he declares. "You can actually push a finger through the worst parts, see?" Mum and I can barely speak as he squashes his index finger right through the spongy wood.

"God, Mum," I whisper finally.

"I had absolutely no idea," she croaks.

Bill nods smugly, crossing his arms as if to say, *I told you so.* "Anyway," he adds, "you're pretty lucky really. She might have sunk in the night and the two of you could have drowned."

"I wouldn't call us lucky," I snap back. As Mum fixes me with a stern look, I know better than to say anything else.

When Charlie has finished work for the day – he paints signs for shops and cafes – he turns up in his beaten-up truck at the boatyard. Mum has already called him, so he knows all about Promise. "Hey," Bella says, jumping out and giving me a heartfelt hug. "Dad told me what's happened. That's awful."

I nod, not knowing what to say, but glad she's here anyway. As we drive back to our stretch of river (I can't say "home" now, can I?), Mum tries to be brave, saying, "Promise had a good, long life. Nothing can go on for ever, can it?" I know she wants to seem strong, for my sake. I also know she feels as crushed as I am, and will be dreading telling Ryan when we get back. As usual, my big brother's phone has been switched off all day, so she hasn't been able to reach him.

"What'll happen to Promise, Helen?" Charlie asks gently.

On the back seat beside me, Bella squeezes my hand.

"She'll be taken to a scrapyard," Mum says flatly. "Bill says he might be able to use some of the timbers and engine parts, so he won't charge us for having her taken away."

"God," I mutter, staring down at my knees. "What'll we do, Mum – buy another boat?"

She shakes her head. I feel silly for asking, because we never have any cash to spare and I know we can't possibly buy a new boat, not on the money Mum earns from her part-time job. That means we can't afford to rent a flat either – anyway, there are hardly any around here. It's all pretty rose-covered cottages and grand country homes. "We're going to be homeless," I mutter to Bella, my eyes filling up with tears.

"Don't be crazy," she whispers back. "You can live with us."

"You know you can all stay with us for as long as you need to," Charlie says, glancing back at me in the rear-view mirror.

"Thanks, Charlie," Mum replies.

"And if there's anything else Kate and I can do to help, Helen," he adds. "We're always there for you and the kids – you know that."

Mum nods but doesn't speak. "It'll be nice, having you staying with us," Bella says, but that doesn't make me feel any better.

I'm still feeling stunned as we arrive at the river and climb on to Bella's boat. Kate hugs us, and Ryan charges over the bridge from Tyler's boat to find out what's going on. "Why all the hugging?" he laughs. His face soon crumples as Mum fills him in on our day. "But . . . what about our stuff?" he blurts out. "How will we get it all from the boatyard?"

"Never mind that," I snap. "What about our *home*, Ryan? Don't you care?"

He frowns, and a flicker of guilt darkens his brown eyes. Perhaps he really is craving a bigger, more comfortable home than Promise could ever be. "We'll have to go and collect it as soon as we can," Mum tells him patiently. "I'll hire a van. God knows where we'll store everything, though. . ."

"We can help you pack up," Bella says.

"Yes, of course we can," Kate adds, "and you can keep all your things here for as long as you need to."

"But where are we going to *live*, Mum?" I interrupt. "We can't stay on Tarragon for ever, can we?"

She meets my gaze. "Look, I promise we'll sort something out. But in the meantime, aren't we lucky to have such great friends?"

"Yeah," I say, hoping I sound like I mean it, because I really do. It's hard to feel truly grateful, though.

Sure, we have friends and somewhere to stay. But a few feet away, there's just an empty space where Promise used to be.

CHAPTER
Four

As life on a boat is usually slow and dreamy, what happens next feels dizzying. "Things are falling into place," Mum tells me and Ryan, after seven nights of us sleeping squished up side by side on cushions on Tarragon's living room floor. At least, Mum and I have been. Ryan has been staying on Tyler and Jake's barge on the opposite riverbank.

"So what's happening?" I ask, stroking Murphy, who's curled up at my side on Bella's deck. It's a baking hot afternoon, far too nice to be cooped up indoors.

"Well, it seems as if our luck's changing," Mum says. "You know Tony at work?"

I nod. He owns the country hotel and lets Mum bring home any leftover cakes at the end of the day. "Well," she continues, "he's friends with some guy who runs a pub. This mate of his is desperate for a chef – his old one walked out last week. Completely left his friend in the lurch, Tony said, so he's pretty desperate. There's a flat, too – it comes with the job."

"A flat?" I gawp at Ryan in horror. He just looks neutral, as if he's taking it all in.

"That's right," Mum says. "I've already spoken to the pub guy and his wife. They said they can't believe I've turned up like this, at exactly the right time. Tony's given me a glowing reference so they're keen for me to start as soon as I can."

We sit in silence for a moment. Bella and her parents are down below deck, making dinner, giving us the chance to talk things over. "So where is this pub?" Ryan asks.

"Er . . . it's in London," Mum replies.

"What?" I exclaim. "We can't go to *London*! I thought you meant somewhere around here, so we'd still be near everyone. . ."

Mum shakes her head. I can tell she's been trying to come across all positive and enthusiastic, but now she's faltering a bit. "Sorry, love, I know it'll be a huge change for all of us. . ."

I look across the river at the row of brightly painted boats, wondering if this is happening for real. It feels as if one minute I was cycling home on that last day of term, the sun blazing in the sky and bunting flapping in the trees, and the next, we've not only lost our home, but we're moving to London, where we don't know a soul. "The pub's in a pretty nice area," Mum continues, though I'm barely listening now. "Can't say I know it, but I'm sure you'll both like it once we're settled in. There'll be lots more for you to do—"

"This is just temporary, right?" I swing round to face her.

Mum hesitates. "I honestly don't know, Josie. I'd love to say yes, but I don't want to lie to you. All I can tell you is, we desperately need somewhere to live, and I seem to have found a job that comes with a flat – we won't even have to pay rent."

"It sounds like a pretty good deal," Ryan adds cautiously.

I study my brother, realizing that, while he's trying not to show it, he's actually intrigued about the prospect of living in London, in a flat – starting a whole new life. Like he's almost looking forward to it. "I know we'll miss everyone," Mum adds, "but it might be better for us as a family. You know how hard it's been for me to find work these past few years. There are so few jobs around here, and in London I should never be out of work."

I clear my throat awkwardly. "D'you mean . . . this is it, Mum? That we'll *never* move back here?" I'm trying to keep the wobble out of my voice.

"Like I said, I just don't know, Josie," Mum says softly.

"But what about our friends and school and everything?"

"Well, it'll be too far for you both to travel to Alcot High, obviously. So, yes, it does mean a new school. I'm sorry. . ."

I put my arms around her. "It's not your fault, Mum. It's the boatyard man's for refusing to fix her—"

"Just leave it, Josie," Ryan mutters.

"It *is*, though! We never had any problems with Promise before, did we?" My voice cracks, but I *won't* cry, not here on Bella's deck.

"We just need to be positive, OK?" Mum says, pulling a brave smile.

"Yeah." Ryan gives my arm a squeeze. "We don't have any choice, and anyway, it means I'll have a better chance of finding a summer job."

"Who cares about that?" I shoot back. "You've never had one before."

"Yeah, because I was too young. I'm sixteen now—"

"OK, I *know* how old you are, you don't have to—"

"Stop bickering, you two," Mum barks at us. "It's not helping at all."

I glare at my brother, deciding there must be a lump of rock where his heart should be. Yet . . . he's right that we don't seem to have any choice. There have been so many things I've wanted to do these past few days – like call Bill from the boatyard and tell him he's *got* to fix Promise, or at least give her back to us, so I can phone around and find someone who's at least willing to try. But I can't, can I? Everything's been decided. This is the end of our life on the river, at least for now. I can't believe it's for ever, though. There must be *something* we can do. . .

The three of us fall into silence as I stroke the warm, wiry top of Murphy's head. "Er ... there's another thing," Mum adds, pushing back her hair distractedly. "I'm really sorry, but the couple who own the pub and flat above it – I'm afraid they don't allow pets."

CHAPTER
Five

Just like Mum said, I'm trying to be positive. Murphy's only having a *holiday* on Tarragon — at least, that's what I keep telling myself. Of course I'll miss him like crazy, but hopefully he'll like it here. Bella has always wanted a dog, so she's bound to spoil him rotten. As for being parted from my best friend, I'm still hanging on to the hope that we'll come back. Maybe someone will see Promise sitting there, looking all forlorn in Bill McIntyre's yard, and decide she's worth saving. They could fix her up and perhaps one day, we'll have enough money to buy her back...

Far-fetched, I know. But I have to keep believing that *something* good will happen.

"There's no need for you to hire a van, Helen," Charlie says later when we're all lounging about on huge cushions on Tarragon's deck, making the most of the evening sunshine. "It'll cost a fortune. We can use my truck — Kate and I will help you."

"No, you've both done more than enough for

us," Mum says firmly, sipping from a chipped mug of tea. "I've found a cheap van-hire place, and I can drop it off at their London depot once we've moved in."

Kate sighs loudly. "I wish you'd let us help you, Helen."

"Well," Mum says, "maybe you could help me pack up at the boatyard. I'm sure I'll appreciate some moral support that day."

"Of course we will," Kate says. "So when is it happening?"

"Er . . . later this week." Mum casts me a quick, anxious glance. She's acting weird – kind of cagey, as if she doesn't want to discuss the details in front of me. Murphy certainly knows something's wrong, as he's been pressed up against my side all evening. As dusk starts to fall, Charlie lights the candles inside glass lanterns, as it's still warm enough for us to sit outside. "So . . . what day are we actually moving, Mum?" I ask hesitantly.

"I'm not quite sure yet, Josie. Um . . . I'm just going to grab a sweater, OK? It's getting chilly out here." Sure – it's only the warmest night of the year so far. She heads down into the cabin, followed by Kate and Charlie, and I frown at Bella as the three of them start mumbling down there.

"What's going on?" Bella hisses.

"I've no idea," I say, desperate to follow them downstairs

but also knowing I'm not wanted right now.

"They're acting really weird." She scowls. "This is so tough for you."

"I'm OK," I say, managing a smile, even though my heart feels as heavy as stone. "I don't know what I'd do if you weren't here, though." My eyes prickle with tears.

"Hey, don't cry," Bella says gently. "London's not that far, and we'll always stay in touch, won't we?"

"Of course we will," I say firmly, pulling Murphy on to my lap.

Across the river, Ryan is playing a rowdy card game with Tyler and Jake. Their laughter floats over the water as if this were just an ordinary day at the start of a long, hot summer.

Bright sunshine beats down on the boats next morning, making those with steel decks almost too hot to walk on. On the roof of Mucky Duck, Maggie and Phil's barge, you can actually fry an egg. They call everyone over to watch, cracking one on to the flat metal surface so we can watch it sizzle. Dragonflies skim the river, their wings gleaming green and blue like jewels. "Let's go swimming," Bella suggests, and minutes later we're all cycling along the twisting lane we take to school – that's me, Bella and Ryan, plus Tyler and Jake – until we reach the woods, where a narrow mossy track leads us down to the lake.

This is the first time we've got around to coming here

since last summer, and it feels far better than moping about on Bella's boat. All of us have been paddling and swimming here for years. Of course, when we were younger, parents would come too. I can remember Dad telling us kids to gather up all the wood we could find, and we'd build a fire and make a sort of grill out of wire for cooking the burgers we'd brought.

As the soft, spongy path curves down towards the water, I glance back at Tyler, who's cycling behind me. This time last year, I'd been hit smack-bang by a crush on him that overwhelmed me for the whole summer. Imagine – falling for one of my brother's friends. Of course Ryan found out – he'd heard me and Bella giggling about it as we swam – and told Tyler right away. It was officially the most embarrassing day of my life, with Ryan, Tyler and Jake all screeching with laughter, and me having to spend virtually the whole time freezing my butt off in the water, because I couldn't face sitting with them on the blankets we'd laid out. Finally, when I'd plucked up the courage to come out – just before my blood turned to ice, basically – I discovered they'd flung my clothes up into the trees. There, snagged on a spindly branch, were my horribly babyish candy-pink knickers, wafting gently like the bunting we had at our party last week. I'd wrapped myself in a giant towel until Bella had finally managed to get them down for me.

As the memory starts to burn my face, I stop my bike

and prop it against a tree.

"Hey." Tyler had appeared at my side, looking, shall we say . . . *sorry*. Not that I'm the kind of girl who holds a grudge for an entire year, especially as I've seen him virtually every day since then.

"Hey," I reply.

As he props up his bike too, I notice he's blushing. "Bit late, I know," he murmurs, "but I'm sorry about that, uh . . . thing last summer."

I smile. "S'all right. I'm over it now."

"Dumb thing to do." He grins awkwardly, and I catch Bella giving us quick look before she darts into the woods. I scamper off to join her, so we can strip down to our swimming costumes in private.

In fact, the day turns out better than I could have hoped for. Messing around in the lake lifts my spirits, and it feel so good, swimming through the cool, clear water in the baking sun.

"Tyler's been hanging around you today," Bella remarks later with a grin.

"Has he?"

"Don't pretend you haven't noticed."

The two of us are laughing as we dry off on towels, then stretch out, exhausted after swimming for hours. "Well," I say, "it's been good, all being together today."

Tyler wanders over and plonks himself down beside us. "We'll all miss you, you know," he says shyly.

I turn towards him and smile, shielding my eyes

against the late afternoon sun. "I'll miss you, too. I'll miss *everyone*," I add quickly, "but I'm sure we'll be back some day." He nods, his pale blue eyes meeting mine. It strikes me that, if this had been last summer, I would have been so excited right now, wondering if this meant the start of something.

Now, though, it feels like an ending.

I swallow hard, wondering how to fill the small silence, when my mobile rings. As I take it out of my bag, I see it's Mum calling. "Hi, Josie?" comes her slightly breathy voice.

"Mum? Everything OK?"

"Yes, sweetheart . . . are you still at the lake?"

"Uh-huh. . ." I glance towards the water's edge, where Ryan, Bella and Jake are piling up wood to make a fire, just like Dad's. Tyler is still sitting on the towel beside me, his face turned biscuit-brown by the sun.

"Josie. . ." Mum pauses. "Er . . . maybe I should have told you. But I thought I was doing the right thing. . ."

"What is it, Mum?"

She clears her throat. "While you've all been at the lake, Charlie took me to pick up the van, and we've spent all morning taking everything off Promise. . ."

My heart lurches. "Have you?"

"Yes, sweetheart. I . . . I'd been thinking it over and I knew it would upset you to be there while we were packing up – and Ryan too. I thought we'd be better doing it when you were having a lovely day with your friends."

"Oh." I blink into the sunshine as a terrible realization washes over me. "So where are you now? Still at the boatyard?"

"Um . . . no," Mum says in a small voice. "We're back at Tarragon. But as soon as you and Ryan get here, we'll be saying our goodbyes and heading off to our new flat."

"But we can't!" I cry, not caring that Tyler is staring at me, or that, down by the lake's edge, the others are all giving me confused looks. "We can't go today," I hiss. "There's . . . there's something on the boat I have to get."

"Hon, we took everything," Mum insists. "Everything that could be moved, I mean. We couldn't bring your mirror, I'm afraid — it was impossible to get it off the wall of your cabin. But I promise I'll buy you a new one."

I let out a huge, desperate gulp.

"It's only a mirror, Josie," Mum says.

I nod wordlessly, swiping at tears with my fingers. Bella has run towards me with Ryan and Jake in pursuit. Everyone gathers around me, asking, *What's wrong? What is it?* I shake my head and turn away. "We need to go back to the boatyard," I tell Mum. "We have to go there today, OK? It's really important."

"Darling, we can't. Promise is being taken to the scrapyard this afternoon. Bill said he desperately needed the space."

"So . . . she's gone already?" I croak.

"Probably, yes," Mum murmurs. "I'm sorry, Josie. I just thought it would be less upsetting this way." I finish the call without saying goodbye.

"What's wrong?" Bella asks, eyes wide with concern.

I look down at the parched ground. "Mum and your parents have been to the boatyard to take all our things off Promise," I say quietly. "We're actually leaving today."

"What? You mean they've emptied the whole boat?" Ryan exclaims.

I nod, aware of everyone's eyes fixed on me.

"They've taken *everything*?" Bella hisses.

I shake my head briefly, meaning *No, not everything. . .* Ryan comes over and puts an arm around my shoulders. "Listen, sis," he says gently, "we'll be OK. We've just got to hold it together for Mum, all right?"

I nod, thinking, *What about Dad?* "What d'you think will happen to Promise at the scrapyard?"

Ryan shrugs. "Dunno. I guess she'll be broken up, maybe sold off as spare parts."

"Where is the yard, anyway?"

He blows out air. "How should I know? There's probably loads. Anyway, listen – we'd better forget about lighting the fire and just head back."

I nod, checking my phone as it bleeps. It's a text from Mum: *Sorry about yr mirror hon, will get you a new one asap.*

I blink at the screen, lost for words as everyone starts to pack away the blankets into backpacks and gather up the bikes. She thinks that's what I'm upset about – an ancient mirror covered in butterfly stickers that I have to stand on tiptoe to see into. But perhaps it's better that way. Maybe by the time we've cycled back to Bella's boat, I'll have convinced myself that a rusty old tin with a dented lid didn't really matter at all.

CHAPTER
Six

A hired van is parked in a small clearing close to the boats. I can hardly believe it contains virtually everything we own, or that we're actually leaving right now.

"You sure about driving this thing, Mum?" Ryan asks, loading in his bike, then mine, and slamming the van door shut.

"Of course I am," she says defensively.

He looks at me and raises a brow. "This might be . . . *interesting*," he whispers, and despite everything, I smile. Although we haven't had a car for ages, we both know that Mum isn't the world's greatest driver.

"Let's make this quick, sweetheart," Mum says as we make our way along the path to say our goodbyes to our friends on the boats. "I can't bear a long, drawn-out thing, and I'm sure you two don't want that either. It's too sad."

I nod and breathe deeply, trying to calm the butterflies in my stomach. There are hugs and good-lucks from

Bella's parents, and some boysy backslapping and high-fives among Ryan and his mates. In fact, *all* the boaters gather to see us off. My eyes are brimming up with tears, and so no one can see, I bob down to make a big fuss of Murphy. "Enjoy your holiday," I whisper, cuddling his furry little body. "I'll come back and see you very soon."

That's how I get through it. You see, I'm still trying to convince myself we're just off on some trip, not moving for good. I'm clinging on to the hope that, by some miracle, Promise won't be broken up at the scrapyard after all, and that one day we'll find her again, as good as new. My tin will still be there in the secret space under my bed, and Dad won't even know we've been gone.

Everyone stands chatting on the riverbank as we prepare to leave. "It'll be cool living above a pub," Tyler says, shuffling about, as if he doesn't quite know what to do with himself.

I look at those pale blue eyes that set my heart alight last summer, when he barely registered my existence. "Hmm," I say. "Well, I hope so."

"Better than this boring place, anyway," he adds, but we both know he doesn't mean it.

He gives me a quick hug, then melts away into the background with Ryan and Jake. Bella throws her arms around me, then slips the silver ring from her finger – the magpie ring I found twinkling in the grass. "You have this," she whispers.

"I can't!" I gasp. "It's your lucky charm."

"But I *want* you to have it. Please, Josie. You found it, it's yours."

I look at her, knowing why she's giving it to me – because I've lost the only memories I have of Dad. I smile, taking it from her and slipping it on to my little finger. It's a twisted coil of silver and fits perfectly. "Thanks. . ." I blink back hot tears.

"It's so you won't forget me," she says with a grin.

"Are you crazy? Of course I won't! You'll come and visit, won't you? Mum says you can, as soon as we're settled in."

"Can't wait," she says.

Mum's putting an arm around me now, saying, "Come on, darling, let's go."

There are more hugs and shouted good-lucks as we leave, and when I glance back, Murphy is darting all over Bella's deck in a light brown blur. Bella picks him up, waggling his paw in a doggy wave, trying to make me laugh. Although I've managed to fix on a fake, brave smile, I feel as if my heart could shatter to pieces as I climb into the van.

CHAPTER
Seven

You'll never guess what our pub is called. Clue: it's not pretty-sounding like "The Swan" or "The Boaters' Retreat", like the ones up the river from where Promise was moored. "It's called 'the Bald-faced Stag'," Mum announces, peering down at the Post-it note with scribbled directions that she's stuck to the van's dashboard.

"What kind of name is that?" I ask from the back seat, wishing she'd keep her eyes on the road while she's driving instead of wobbling all over the place. "Why does it have a bald face? Is there something wrong with it?"

Mum chuckles and shakes her head. "I've no idea, Josie."

"Stop firing questions," Ryan snorts from the passenger seat, pulling out his headphones. "It's just the name of the pub. It doesn't *mean* anything." I glare at a spot on the back of his neck, wondering why he insisted on sitting in the front of the van when he's hardly said a word so far. If I was next to Mum, we'd be chatting away, trying to take our minds off the fact that we'd just left our home and friends behind, and are heading to part of London we've never been to before. "I *know* it's the pub's name," I reply calmly. "I'm not a complete idiot, Ryan. I sort of get the idea that there aren't herds of deer roaming about in the middle of London."

"Yes, OK, Josie," Mum snaps. Great — now she's ratty, too. What have I done, exactly?

I blink at Ryan's spot. It's a pretty impressive one. It should have contours to show how high it is, like a hill on a map. "Mum. . ."

"*Please* don't keep going on at me, Josie. . ."

What's she talking about now? We're moving, aren't we? Surely it's natural to have a few questions. "You know how our flat's above the pub?" I say meekly.

"*Yes*, love," Mum says with exaggerated patience.

"Well . . . it will be separate, won't it? I mean, people won't be able to just wander upstairs and see where we live, will they?"

"Of course it'll be separate," she says firmly. "It'll be our home, just like Promise was."

Hmmm. Well, not *quite*.

The hills and fields have ended now, making way for the suburbs where every house looks the same (I don't think I've *ever* seen two boats looking remotely alike).

Then things become grubbier, with the buildings and odd patch of scrubby grass looking as if they need a good hosing down on this warm, dusty afternoon. I don't want you to think I've led such a sheltered, watery life that I've never seen a tower block or a traffic jam before, or that I'd faint at the sight of a Topshop. But for regular stuff like shopping, the cinema and going for haircuts, we always went to Braidford, a medium-sized town a twenty-minute bus ride from where we lived. London feels *huge* to me. It was always for special occasions only, like birthday outings, or a Christmas shopping trip – like when Mum and I came on our own to buy Ryan a metal detector. He'd desperately wanted one that year, the first Christmas since Dad died. And, although we were broke as usual, Mum was determined to make our Christmas extra-special.

It was a brilliant day, just the two of us. We had time to talk, which is hard when you live on the river and everyone is hopping on and off each other's boats all the time. I asked her about Dad, and why he'd died, and for the first time she explained that no one really knew. The pneumonia he'd had that year might have weakened his heart, or there could have been something wrong with it all along, even with all the running he'd done. A bit like Promise – none of us had known that things we couldn't see were secretly going very wrong.

It's funny, but even talking about Dad didn't bring

down our mood that day as we lugged the metal detector, and the bike I'd chosen, back on to the train. Today is, shall we say, slightly *less* brilliant, especially as I'm now obsessed with Ryan's spot watching me, like a grumpy, unblinking eye.

As I look out of the van's smeary side window, there's no massive shopping mall like the one Mum and I went to. Just row after row of grey terraced houses which don't even have front gardens, just dusty pavements with litter lying about. "Are we nearly there?" I ask, noticing Mum glancing down at the Post-it note.

"Um . . . I'm sure it's somewhere around here," she replies.

"That means we're lost," I say under my breath.

"No, we're not. . ." She takes a corner too fast, causing a pile of boxes to tumble down in the back of the van.

"Whoa – steady, Mum," Ryan cries.

"Thank you, Ryan, I *do* know how to drive. . ."

Hmmm. I've just thought of an eighth wonder of the world – the fact that Mum ever managed to pass a driving test.

"I just mean, if we *were* lost," I say carefully, "you could stop, and I could have a walk about and look for Castle Street."

"You can't walk about around here by yourself," Mum exclaims.

"But. . ." I frown, wondering if she's forgotten something important. "We *are* going to be living here.

I'll be walking around all the time, Mum."

"Yes, well, that's different."

"Or we could *all* get out," I suggest, "and have a look around together."

"We can't leave the van by itself," Mum shrieks, "with all our stuff in!"

"Yeah," Ryan growls, twisting round to face me, "I think we've had enough of your suggestions for one day."

"I only made two," I growl back, brightening as a sign comes into view – a pub sign, sticking out from a scruffy old building, with possibly the worst painting of a stag I've ever seen in my life (not that I've seen many). "There it is!" I shout, just before Mum pulls up outside a big brown, glossy door and turns off the engine. Wordlessly, the three of us clamber out of the van and stare at the pub, which takes up virtually the whole block.

"It's huge," Ryan marvels.

"It looks more like a hotel," I murmur.

"I think it was at some point," Mum says. "It's not any more, obviously." We all stand there for a moment, as if nervous about going inside. There are loads of windows with the kind of dimply glass you can't see through, and window boxes and hanging baskets with flowers in. They all look shrivelled up, though, as if no one has watered them for a very long time. As for the stag – even I could paint a better one than this, and animals have never been my strong point. It looks more like a pony, wearing fake antlers as a joke.

I'm still gazing up at the sign, hardly believing we'll be living here, as Mum puts her arms around Ryan and me. "So," she says with an unsteady smile, "what d'you think of our new home?"

CHAPTER
Eight

Before either of us has a chance to answer, a man with a round, shaved head and an enormous stomach encased in a tight stripy T-shirt has bounded out of the pub to greet us. "I assume you're Helen?" he asks with a big grin.

"Yes, that's me," Mum replies. "This is Ryan, Josie. . ."

"I'm Vince. Great to meet you all." He shakes Mum's hand, then Ryan's and mine, almost crushing my skinny fingers in his overenthusiastic grasp. "I'm *so* glad to see you guys," he continues in his big, booming voice. "Your mum here – you know what she is?"

I smile meekly and shake my head.

"An angel," Vince declares. "I've never hired a live-in member of staff without meeting face-to-face before. But you just know, don't you, when the right person turns up?" He laughs and grips Mum's arm. "You're a lifesaver, Helen. Anyway, come in, let me show you around. . ."

He pushes open the pub door and the three of us troop in behind him. I should probably say it's lovely, and I'm excited to be here – but all I can think is, this is *nothing* like those pretty riverside pubs where we'd go occasionally for a treat.

They'd have big, airy windows and soft music playing, and there'd be delicious foody smells. This room is huge – far bigger than any pub I've ever been into – but feels grubby and neglected. You can see dust dancing in shafts of sunlight from the grimy windows, and a stale, beery smell hangs in the air. There are wooden tables dotted around the edges of the room, and a long, polished wooden bar that seems to go on forever. A couple of old greasy-haired men are sitting there on stools, mumbling together – at least, they *were* mumbling. Now we've walked in, they've swung around and are staring as if we're all stark naked. "Hi!" Mum says in an over-bright voice.

"This is Helen," Vince announces, "our wonderful new chef."

Mum beams hopefully at the two men, who turn away and start chatting again. She looks back at Vince. "It's very, um . . . quiet in here, isn't it?" she ventures.

"Still early," Vince says. "By half-eight the place'll be packed. Anyway, I need to introduce you, get you settled in. . . Maria!" he shouts, and a woman with obviously dyed hair – not blonde but actually *gold* – appears, all smiles, from the back room.

"Oh, you've arrived! Welcome, welcome," she says, engulfing us all with her sweet perfume cloud. "I'm Maria, Vince's wife. We're so excited to have you here." She turns, shouts, "Chantelle!" and waits expectantly, but no one comes. "Chantelle!" Maria calls again, rolling her eyes and laughing huskily. "Excuse our daughter's rudeness. No manners, has she, Vince?"

Vince smiles and shakes his head. "She'll be helping you, Helen. Bit of an attitude, so don't take any cheek from her." While Mum tries not to look startled, Vince and Maria both chuckle fondly as if this was the *cutest* thing. "I'm sure she'll be happy to show you around, Josie," Vince adds kindly. "How old are you again, love?"

"Thirteen," I reply.

"Well, Chantelle's just turned fourteen," Maria says, patting her weird gold hair, which is so heavily sprayed, it looks crispy. "I'm sure the two of you will be best mates in no time."

"Er, yes," I say, hoping it sounds convincing.

"Chantelle!" Maria shouts again, causing the two old men to flinch. "Come out here and be friendly." Still nothing.

Then, as Maria and Vince fall back into conversation with Mum, something catches my eye. No, not something – *someone*. Behind the bar, a door leads to a brightly lit back room, presumably the kitchen, and in that doorway a girl has appeared. She has a tough, pale face, hard as a marble, and her mouth is set in a sneer. Her blonde hair is pulled back tightly, and her eyes narrow and fix directly on mine, as if challenging me. As if saying, *Who do you think you are, moving in here?*

I'm vaguely aware of Vince chatting to Ryan as my gaze slides back to the girl.

She's still looking at me, her skin almost luminous, her dark eyes heavily rimmed with black liner. And the only thing I can think of is . . . to *smile*. For courage, I roll Bella's ring between my thumb and index finger, and then I fix on what I hope passes for a confident grin. For a moment, she looks confused. Then, in a flash, she disappears back into the kitchen.

"Like I said, Helen," Maria is saying, her metallic bangles jingling, "me and Vince are around pretty much all of the time, if there's anything you need to know. I hope you'll all be very happy here." She beams at us. "I have to say, we'd almost lost hope of ever finding anyone to replace Kevin. . ."

"Can't get a chef to stay here," Vince adds, while Maria throws him a quick, irritated look.

"Why?" The word pings out of my mouth, and everyone turns to stare at me.

"Why what, sweetheart?" Maria asks.

"Um . . . why does no one stay?" I'm aware of Mum and Ryan shooting me irritated looks.

"It's just . . . pretty busy and demanding," Vince says quickly, "but I'm sure you'll cope, Helen."

"Of course I will," Mum replies in her trying-to-sound-confident voice. At least Vince and Maria seem kind, I decide as we all head outside to unload the van. They help us to carry our boxes into the pub, and Vince even gives us bottles of Coke and bags of crisps. Well, I *assume* they're crisps. While everyone else carries the first load of boxes upstairs, I stop in the middle of the pub and rip open my packet. I pluck a crisp from the bag, pop it into my mouth – and immediately spit the hard, salty thing back into my hand, nearly puking all over the blood-coloured carpet. What *are* these things? I check the packet: "Piggy's Pork Scratchings", it says. Ugh. Little bits of pig skin, and I've been vegetarian since I was eight! Glancing around – thank God those two old men have gone – I spot a huge, dusty-looking plant and scuttle over to drop the wet porky thing into its pot. I *like* Vince, and don't want to offend him, so I press it down into the soil and cover it over.

"It won't grow, you know."

The voice makes my heart jolt. I swing round to face that girl – Chantelle – who's smirking at me from behind the bar. "*What* won't grow?" I ask.

"That thing you just planted in Mum's pot." She sniggers, batting coal-black eyelashes and pursing her glossy lips.

I can't understand why she has taken an instant dislike to me, but I'm determined not to react. Fiddling with Bella's ring on my little finger, I manage to meet Chantelle's cool gaze and reply, "Oh well, it's worth a try, isn't it?"

Then I pick up my cardboard box of belongings and, trying to ignore the rustle of the pork scratchings bag in my jeans pocket, I saunter towards the stairs.

CHAPTER

Nine

As I've mentioned, I'm not some wimp from the country who starts trembling when she sees lots of traffic and people milling about. Even so, I have to ask a question here.

Whatever happened to the stars?

I mean, we're still in the same hemisphere, aren't we? This part of London is only an hour and half's drive (Mum-speed) from the stretch of river where I lived all my life, where there were so many stars you couldn't begin to count them. And now, from my bedroom window above the Bald-faced Stag in Castle Street – where, incidentally, there is no castle either – stars are completely, one hundred per cent absent. And, whilst we're talking about absent things, what about the rocking motion that lulled me to sleep all those years in my cabin? Here I am, lying in the first double bed I've ever had in my life, and I'm not thinking, *You're so lucky, Josie Lennox*. No, I'm thinking: *It doesn't move.* This bed is *completely still*. The weird thing is, although I rarely noticed the rocking, I do notice the stillness.

I shouldn't be thinking about this. I should be sleeping soundly after helping to lug our boxes upstairs. But, even though the pub has closed now, and all the customers have gone home (Vince was right – the place was packed tonight), I just can't. I'm out of bed now, standing at my dirty bedroom window, looking out at the city and the glow it makes in the sky, like orangey ink spreading upwards. Has this glow blotted out the stars? Are they all still there, like when you scrape black wax crayon off a picture with a fingernail to expose the fiery colours underneath?

Mum's right – I ask way too many questions. For instance: pork scratchings. What are they all about? Who had the brilliant idea of gathering together all the tough bits of pig skin that no one wanted and putting them in little red and gold bags? And what'll I do if Vince offers me them again?

Oh no. Now I've started thinking of questions, they just won't stop. Like:

How long are we going to be here for? Will the stale foody smell in our flat ever go away, or will I just stop noticing it? And what about Chantelle? She seems to despise me, for some reason. . . I'm mulling all of this over when my bedroom door creaks open.

"Hey," Mum says softly, stepping into my room. "It's nearly one in the morning, sweetheart. What are you doing out of bed?"

I shrug. "Just looking out."

She smiles and joins me at the window, glancing back at my room with its horrible speckled mustard walls. "So you haven't started unpacking your things yet," she remarks, meaning the boxes piled up against one wall, as yet untouched.

"Er . . . no. Actually, I was thinking, it's probably best if I don't."

"Why's that?" she asks with a frown.

"I just don't think there's much point. I mean . . . this place has all the stuff we need – all the furniture and even cutlery in the kitchen. We don't want to muddle up our personal stuff with the things that belong to the flat, do we?"

Mum brushes a strand of dark hair from my face. "It doesn't matter if our things get mixed up, Josie," she says softly.

"Yeah, but it'll be easier for us to leave quickly," I explain, "if we keep our own stuff in the boxes."

That's when she gives me a really intense look, and says, "Josie. . ." Then her eyes fill with tears and she stops abruptly. "Come through and sit in the kitchen with me."

She leads me there, as if I couldn't find my own way down the corridor with its beige walls and doors to all the other bedrooms (there are six of them, plus two bathrooms and a living room – this place is *huge*). "You think it's not worth us unpacking," Mum starts, switching on the kettle, "because we'll only be staying for a short while, right?"

"Yeah." I nod. That's me, ever practical.

"Josie, love. . ." She rubs at her tired eyes. "I don't know how long we're going to be here, OK, but it's *not* temporary. You know you'll be starting school here in the autumn. . ."

"Yes, but—"

"We can't think of it like, like . . . we're just here for a few weeks."

"But eventually," I cut in, "we might be able to save up enough money and get another boat—"

"There are no plans to get another boat," Mum says, reaching across the table to clasp my hand. "I'm sorry, darling, but those days are over. I need to work full time now, and this is our home. . ."

"It's *not* our home!" I jump up from my chair, sending it clattering against an ancient dented fridge behind me. "I'm miles away from Bella and Murphy and we don't know anyone here. *And* it smells horrible. . ." Mum gets up and tries to hug me, but I push her away. "Leave me alone!"

"Josie," she says firmly. "Listen to me. We'll just have to make the best of it, OK? We have a huge flat – you must admit, we were so cramped on Promise. . ."

"I didn't mind," I grumble.

"Well," she says briskly, handing me a cup of tea, "this is the best I can do for us right now. I need to look after you and Ryan and there's no one else to help us."

"What about Grandma and Grandpa?" I ask.

Mum presses her lips together. I mean Dad's parents — Mum's died before I was born — who live in New Zealand. As far as I can work out, Mum was never their favourite person. They reckoned it was her crazy idea to raise Ryan and me on a boat (actually true). And, according to them, it was also her fault that Dad caught the pneumonia which might have caused his heart problems (of *course* that wasn't anything to do with Mum. When I was a bit older, she explained to me that they were hurting too, and just needed someone to blame). Anyway, my grandparents were so angry and upset that they left England and moved as far away from us as it's possible to be.

"Sorry, Mum," I say quietly, when she still hasn't replied.

She raises a faint smile and brings the mug to her lips. "It's OK, love, but I don't think Grandma and Grandpa are likely to come running to our rescue any time soon."

"We don't need them," I say firmly, ashamed of my outburst.

"All *I* need," she says, squeezing my hand, "is for the three of us to be together and as strong as we can be."

I nod and sip my hot, sweet tea.

"So," she goes on, "can we make a bargain, Josie? That we'll try and look on the bright side from now on?"

I mull this over, wondering how I'll do this when I'm already missing Bella and Murphy like crazy, not to mention the only home I've ever known. "I'll try," I say quietly.

Mum smiles, her eyes glinting in the dim kitchen light. "You're an amazing girl," she says, getting up from her seat and planting a kiss my forehead. "Now, back to bed, OK?"

Stifling a yawn, I hug her, then pad quietly down the stale-smelling corridor to my room. But instead of climbing straight into bed, I pause by my window again, thinking maybe, if I look hard enough, there'll be a star. Just one will do, to remind me that they're still out there somewhere.

I keep looking until something catches my eye. With a gasp, I realize there's a *boy* out there, all alone in the street, standing astride a bike. He's looking up at me. My God – he can see me in my black and white spotty Dalmatian pyjamas! Heart pounding, I jump back and lurk in the shadowy darkness of my room. How long was I standing there, and how long was he staring up? Is that what people do around here for fun – cycle around in the middle of the night, peering into people's windows? That makes him sound creepy, but in fact, he isn't at all. He has a mop of dark hair, a sweet, inquisitive face, and is making no move to cycle away. Although I can still watch him, I don't think he can see me. I moisten my dry lips with my tongue, trying to muster the courage to walk back towards the window, and maybe make eye contact with him. I sort of want to. There's something intriguing about him, like he could actually be a friend. What would I do, though — smile and wave? Or force open the heavy old window and ask why he's roaming about at half-one in the morning? He'd probably laugh and zoom away.

I take a step forward. The boy is looking around, clearly in no particular hurry to go anywhere. I step forward again, wondering where he lives and what his name is — maybe he's a neighbour, or goes to the school Ryan and I will be starting in September. This is dumb, I realize; there are tons of schools in London and anyway, Mum hasn't managed to finalize which one we're going to yet. I'll probably never see this boy again. The weird thing is, I *want* to. I want to know what brings him out to the city streets at night.

Taking a deep breath, I make my way back towards my window. Seeing me there, the boy raises a hand in a sort of wave, and his face bursts into the sweetest, cheekiest grin I've ever seen in my life.

Then he's gone.

I blink down at the space he's left, wondering who he is and whether he'll come back, if I wait long enough. Down at the end of the corridor, I hear Mum switching off the kitchen light and making her way past my door to her own bedroom. "I hope you're in bed, Josie," she says as she passes.

What can I say — "Er, no, Mum, but listen, an amazing thing's just happened"? I can still picture the boy's incredibly cute, open face and, despite everything that's happened these past few days, the thought of him lifts my heart.

As quietly as I can, I tiptoe across the worn chocolate-brown carpet, slip into the creaky old bed with its lumpy mattress and pull the sheets around me. "Josie?" Mum calls out softly.

"I'm going to sleep now," I reply.

"OK. Goodnight, love."

As her footsteps fade away, I breathe in deeply, aware of a faint wood-smokey smell. Where is *that* coming from? I realize then that it's the scent of the logs we burnt on our cast-iron stove on Promise. Somehow, even though we hadn't lit it since spring, the smell has followed us to London. I close my eyes and inhale it, hoping it never fades away.

Then something new flickers into my mind, as bright and warming as a flame. It's that boy on the bike, smiling up at me. As I drift towards sleep in my strange new home, my head is filled with stars.

CHAPTER
Ten

I wake up next morning thinking, *Was he for real?* Slipping out of bed, I pad across my room, past the tatty white wardrobe and wonky chest of drawers, and peer down to the street. Of course the boy hasn't come back. The only person out there is Vince, with another tight, stripy T-shirt stretched over his belly as he unloads crates from a van.

By the time I've fixed myself a bowl of Cheerios – Ryan isn't up yet, and I guess Mum must be down in the pub kitchen already – I've remembered her "look on the bright side" line. Maybe I missed its importance last night. It wasn't just a casual request, I realize now as I crunch spoonfuls of cereal. It was a *plea*. She needs both me and Ryan to help her make this work. Glancing around the kitchen at the murky brown cupboards – what is it with the nasty colour obsession in this flat? – I try to figure out precisely how I might make myself feel joyously happy about living here.

OK, there are lots of things we have now that we didn't have on Promise, such as:

- A bath. I have to admit, our old shower – which worked with a whining, battery-powered pump – was pretty pathetic. Like being dribbled on by a kitten, basically. The bath here has yellowy stains and looks as old as the building itself. But it's also massive, probably designed for five Victorians to all splosh around in at once.

- A proper flushing loo instead of one filled with blue chemicals that you have to empty yourself at the sanitary station. That's the place where boaters' toilet stuff goes. We had to chug along the river, tie up at this little concrete building, carry out our loo and tip its contents into this big toilet place. It was never a favourite activity of mine.

- A toaster with many settings (two/four slices, regular/ frozen bread) plus a removable drawer for crumbs. On Promise, we didn't have non-essential appliances like computers or hairdryers, and we didn't have a crumb drawer either. And we were PERFECTLY HAPPY WITHOUT ONE THANK YOU VERY MUCH! Whoops. I forgot our "look on the bright side" pact for a moment. . .

- A proper front door. At least, the pub has one. The door to our actual flat is next to the bar, to the right of the huge flowerpot where my pork scratchings plant will soon burst forth, ha ha. That'll show Princess Chantelle...

– Oh, and my very own double bed! How could I forget that?

I put down my spoon as Ryan appears in the kitchen. Wearing just his boxers, he grabs the milk carton from the table, takes a noisy slurp and slams it back down. "Sleep all right?" he asks, plonking himself on the seat opposite mine.

"Yeah." I nod. "Yeah ... I didn't expect to, but I did."

He grins. "Me too. It's all right, isn't it, having a room that's actually big enough to swing a cat in?"

"We don't have a cat," I remind him.

"Oh, c'mon, Josie. You have to admit, we couldn't live on Promise for ever..."

"*I* thought we could," I exclaim.

"Yeah, well ... things change, don't they?" His eyes darken as he tips an enormous mound of Cheerios into his bowl and sloshes milk all over them.

"I guess so," I reply, stealing a glance at him. I realize now that he's missing his friends – Tyler and Jake especially – and our life on the river, just as I am. Only he's determined to make the best of this, because he knows we have nowhere else to go.

And if my hairy big brother can do that? Well ... I guess I can, too.

*

After checking in with Mum, who's being shown around the pub kitchen by Maria, I head out on my own. I promised Mum I wouldn't venture too far and, although she looked unsure, she could hardly stop me. After all, how else am I supposed to fill the summer? By hanging out in the flat all day? "Maybe Ryan could go with you," she suggested, at which my brother snorted into his hand.

So, here I am, having escaped my mustard bedroom . . . to do what, exactly? Prowl the streets like a cat. It's another hot, airless day, and Bella and the others will probably have cycled to the lake again, and be plunging into the cool water right now. . .

No, I shouldn't be thinking about that.

Instead, I focus hard on looking as if I know where I'm going, rather than wandering aimlessly. I pass a row of dingy terraced houses and a gang of kids and teenagers all messing about on scooters and bikes. Groups of old ladies are chatting and laughing outside a community centre, and a furious-looking woman is pulling a wailing toddler along by the arm.

I'm on the main road now – it's far busier than the side streets around the pub – passing run-down shops with boxes of wilting vegetables outside. On a whim, I turn down a narrow alleyway strewn with bottles and cans. I don't know where I'm going, or what I'm looking for. It's not as if I'll make friends, wandering about on my own. What did Mum say about me getting to know people – that it'll happen naturally when I start school in September? September! That feels like a lifetime away.

Anyway, what will I do then? March up to someone and say, "Hi, my name's Josie"? Is *that* what you do? Or d'you hover around the edges of the school grounds, hoping that someone notices and takes pity? It was easy with boaters. Every so often, a new boat would arrive at our stretch of river, and occasionally that new boat would have kids around my age on it, and we'd become friends. Sometimes they'd move on, and a new family would take their place. It all happened quite naturally.

I stop and look around. The alley has brought me to an old skate park with houses on every side. Every inch of the high walls around it is sprayed with graffiti. There are ramps, railings and a huge concrete bowl thing. There isn't a living thing in sight – not a blade of grass, or even a dusty dandelion poking through a concrete crack. No people either.

Where does everybody go around here? It's the summer holidays. Thousands of kids just like me are off school. What do they *do*? Surely they can't all just hang about the streets all day?

I plonk myself down on one of the ramps. You wouldn't think a great curve of concrete would be comfortable, but it feels like a huge, smooth radiator as I lie back on it. I pull out my phone from the pocket of my shorts and call Bella.

"Josie," she yelps. "You've only been gone a day but it feels like ages already. I miss you so much! What are you doing?"

Hearing her voice makes me smile. "What am I *doing*? Missing you like mad, of course. Oh, and I'm lying on a big concrete ramp in a skate park."

"Right." She laughs. "Well, you'll be glad to know Murphy's OK."

"Is he? He's not pining for me, depressed as hell?"

Bella chuckles kindly. Of course, I don't *want* him to be refusing his food or teetering on the very edge of her deck, as if about to end it all by leaping into the river (he can swim anyway, so that wouldn't work). "I'm sure he *does* miss you," she says diplomatically. "So, anyway, what's your new place like?"

I start to describe the huge old pub with its terrible painted sign and the flat upstairs that used to be a hotel. "Sounds great," Bella says, sounding almost envious.

"Yeah, well, it's not. It's as if someone looked at all the colours in the world and thought – right, let's pick the very worst ones and paint the flat with them."

"Aw," she says with a heavy sigh. "Couldn't you change your bedroom around and ask your mum to do it up for you?"

I turn this possibility over in my mind. "She doesn't have time for that. She's virtually living downstairs in the pub kitchen already, finding out how everything works and what kind of meals the regular customers like best."

There's a small pause, which makes Bella feel horribly

far away. "Have you met anyone yet?" she asks.

"Just Vince and Maria. They own the pub and live a few streets away. They seem like kind, nice people . . . unlike their daughter."

"What's she like?" Bella wants to know.

"Um . . . not exactly friendly. Anyway, listen – last night, I looked out of my bedroom window, and there was this boy in the street, staring up at me."

"Ugh, creepy!" she exclaims.

"No," I say quickly, "it wasn't like that. He looked . . . nice. Sort of lost."

"And this was in the middle of the night?"

"About half-one in the morning, yeah." I bite my lip, knowing how weird this sounds. "Anyway," I add, "what's everyone been up to?"

"You've only been gone a day," she laughs. "You know what it's like around here. *Nothing* ever happens."

"Come on, there must be something."

"Er . . . oh, I know! Tyler and Jake dared each other to wear their mum's swimming costumes and swim from one side of the river to the other in them." Her voice starts shaking with giggles. "You should have seen Tyler in this red and white polka-dot bikini. . ."

I nearly choke with laughter. "No! Did you get pictures?"

"Wish I had, but I couldn't find my phone and it was all over too quickly." She snorts loudly, adding, "He'd never have done it if you were there."

"What d'you mean?" I ask.

"Oh, Josie. . . I'm sure he had a crush on you, you know. It was obvious, that last day we went to the lake."

"The day we were leaving," I mutter.

There's a pause, and I bat away a wasp from my face.

"Rotten timing, I guess," Bella agrees.

"Yeah. So what else has been happening?"

"Uh . . . nothing much. A family on a hired boat had engine problems and moored next to us. . ."

"Where Promise used to be, you mean?" A wave of yearning grips my heart.

"Um . . . yes," she says, "and Dad helped them out and they cooked dinner for us." My vision fuzzes. It all sounds so . . . perfect. It's not Bella's fault; I did ask for news, after all. "Why don't you ask your mum if you can come back and spend at least some of the holidays here?" she suggests, as if tapping into my thoughts. "You can squeeze in with us. Stay as long as you like – for the whole of the holidays if you want to. Mum and Dad would love to have you here. . ."

"Maybe," I tell her. But even as I say it, I know it wouldn't feel right, giving up on the Bald-faced Stag so soon. Like abandoning Mum (and, yes, Ryan too).

"So . . . tell me more about the pub," she urges me.

I try to think of something funny to tell her, but all I can dredge up is a description of biting into what I thought was a strange, thick crisp, but was actually a chunk of piggy skin. "Oh," I add quietly, "and two girls have just walked into the park and they're coming this way."

"Do they look friendly?" she asks.

"Uh – not especially, Bells. Better go."

CHAPTER
Eleven

There's no doubt that the two girls are heading straight towards me. They're halfway across the park now, acting like they're official patrollers of this place and I happen to be trespassing. I'm already working out what to say. . .

I've as much right to be here as you do.

I didn't notice anyone selling entry tickets.

No, you can't have my phone. Are you kidding? It was the cheapest in the shop and my best friend's dad accidentally drove over it with his truck when I left my bag lying on the ground. Look at it now — bent like a boomerang. Throw it and it'd probably come back. Amazingly, though, it still works. . .

All of this sounds far braver than I feel inside. I glance over at the girls, who are both wearing sunglasses, tiny frayed denim skirts and little vest tops (there is some variation here. One top is white, scattered with silvery sparkles, while the other is the precise candy-pink shade that I went the moment I saw my knickers dangling from that tree by the lake). I cross my legs awkwardly on the warm concrete ramp, trying to look as if I belong.

"Hi." The girl in the white sparkly top is right in front of me now, and parks her tiny bum on the ramp beside me.

"Hi," I reply. She whips off her sunglasses and tosses back her long blonde hair. "Oh, it's you," I say as Chantelle-from-the-pub studies me coolly, her lashes so thickly mascara'd it's a wonder she can actually blink.

"Yeah." She smirks. "This is my friend Gemma."

"Hey," Gemma says.

"Hey," I say back, taking in her smoky eyes and poker-straight dark hair with dip-dyed reddish ends. My face is bare, as it always is (the only make-up I own is a lipsalve – does that actually count as make-up?), and I'm wearing a plain navy T-shirt, dark denim shorts and beaten-up canvas lace-ups. Will I ever fit in around here?

Chantelle smirks at her friend. "This is Josie, the one I was telling you about."

"Oh, yeah," Gemma says with a silly laugh. I'm now feeling as relaxed as if I were about to have a tooth pulled out.

"Is that short for something?" Chantelle asks.

"What, you mean my name? Yes – it's short for Josephine." My mouth feels as parched as the concrete all around us.

"Oooh," she sniggers. "That's a funny name."

Is it really? Oddly enough, no one's thought that before. "Yes, well, no one calls me that," I explain.

"Why not?" Gemma asks, narrowing her eyes at me.

"Um . . . I don't really like it."

"Don't blame you," Chantelle snorts. "It's really old-fashioned, isn't it? *Josephine. . .*" She repeats it in a put-on posh voice, and I squirm uncomfortably on the ramp. "Sounds like someone who's about eighty years old!"

"Hahaha," Gemma cackles, and I try to raise a smile to show that I can take a joke, too.

"So which school d'you go to?" Chantelle asks.

I shrug. "I don't know yet. Mum's trying to sort it out with the council."

She blinks those stiff, clumpy lashes. "You used to live on a boat, didn't you?"

"Yeah, that's right. . ." Here we go: *are you a gypsy then? Couldn't your mum afford a house?*

"What, like at sea?" Chantelle giggles. "Is your dad a captain or something? Eww, I'd puke if I lived on a boat. I'd be barfing all day long." She makes a dramatic vomiting noise and they both burst into peals of laughter.

"It wasn't a sea boat," I say firmly. "And my dad's—"

"What did you do about the loo?" Chantelle cuts in.

I blink at her. "Well, we had one on the boat."

"Yeah, but where did it go?"

"Where did *what* go?" I frown at her, really confused now. What's with the obsession with my old loo?

"The poos and wees," Gemma explains. "What happened to all that?"

I'm now faintly distracted, as another life form has entered the park. It's a huge, shaggy black dog with no visible features – like an enormous fluffy cushion with paws. I watch as it nuzzles what I *think* is its front end around an overflowing litter bin. "Did it go in the river?" Chantelle rants on. "Like, did it come out of a pipe and just float there? Ugh – poos in the river." She covers her mouth with her hands. "That's gross!"

The girls are so fixated by all this loo talk, they haven't even noticed the enormous, ownerless hound pottering around the park.

"It didn't go in the river," I say in my most patient voice. "It just stayed in the loo."

"What, like, for ever?" Chantelle gawps at me. I focus on the biggest, blackest mascara clump, wondering if at some point it'll ping off her eyelash, drop on to the concrete and sizzle in the sun.

"Well . . . no. It stayed there, in chemicals, till we went to a special place to empty it."

"Ugh," she shudders, glancing at Gemma. I'm feeling a little less intimidated now. Somehow, the loo conversation has made them both seem pretty ridiculous. I try to imagine them having to empty a chemical loo, or even trying to steer a boat, and can't help smiling to myself.

"Look, Chantelle," Gemma mutters, pointing at

the dog, who's now plonked itself down on the hard concrete ground.

"Oh my God." Chantelle shrinks back. "I hate it when you see a dog with no owner. It could go mad and bite you."

The dog has now stretched itself out, and is basking in the sun. "It doesn't look aggressive," I venture, another smile tweaking my lips.

"Yeah, but how can you tell? It must be a stray. It could be dangerous. Don't dogs sometimes go crazy in the heat?"

I'm trying not to laugh now as Chantelle leaps up, popping her sunglasses back on as if they'll protect her from this clearly savage hound.

"It must be boiling hot," I suggest. "We should get some water from somewhere. . ."

At that, Chantelle tugs hard on Gemma's arm. "I'm not going anywhere near that thing. *You* can if you want. C'mon Gemma, let's go." Their sandals slap against the hard ground as they scurry away, and the park feels oddly still when they've gone.

OK, they could be right. Maybe this dozy hound is really a dangerous beast, who's just working up to ripping my arm out of its shoulder socket. I kind of doubt it, though. I get up and make my way towards it. Now I'm close enough, I can see that it does have a nose (black, shiny) poking out from all that fur, and its tongue is hanging out, too. The poor thing is panting.

I sit on the hot, hard ground beside it and give its head a little stroke. So far, due to its outrageously fluffy coat, I haven't been able to work out if it's a he or a she. "Someone must be really missing you," I say gently, noticing a flash of silver under its chin. It's a little bone-shaped tag, and when I turn it over I can make out a name engraved on it: Daisy. There's a phone number, too. Rather than call right away, I decide to wait, because Daisy has probably run off and her owner will be here any minute. But the longer I sit in the baking heat, the more obvious it seems that no one's going to come. And she desperately needs a drink.

"C'mon, Daisy," I say, ruffling her soft black fur. "We'll find you some water, OK?"

Obediently, she gets up, still panting hard and trotting close to my side as we make for the park's exit. There's a river somewhere around here, Mum said – unbelievably, it eventually joins *our* river, where Promise used to be – but so far, I haven't spotted it. I could take Daisy to the pub (can't bring myself to say "home" yet), but what if Chantelle's gone back there and makes a huge fuss? She's obviously terrified of dogs. Anyway, they're not allowed in the flat, otherwise we'd have Murphy with us, wouldn't we? I glance down at Daisy, wishing she'd magically turn into a little wiry brown terrier, then feel guilty and stop to give her a hug.

We're in the alley now, and Daisy is still showing no sign of wanting to dash off – which is just as well, as I don't have anything I could use as a lead. I crouch down and call the number on her tag, but it goes straight to voicemail: *Hello, you've reached Jane Harper, please leave a message after the tone. . .* The voice is posh, confident, important-sounding.

"Er . . . hello," I say hesitantly. "I've, er, found your dog, Daisy. At least, I think she's yours – this is the number on her collar. I'm, um. . ." I glance around, having just reached the end of the alley. Where am I, exactly? There's no street sign in sight. "Um . . . I'm quite near the Bald-faced Stag," I finish in a rush, wondering why I'm not remotely intimidated by a huge, hairy hound, yet give me an answering machine to talk to and I can hardly string a sentence together.

"So where to now, Daisy?" I ask her, slipping my phone back into my pocket.

She peers at me through her messy black fringe.

"Let's get you some water," I add, turning into the main shopping street. Still showing no sign of sinking her teeth into me, Daisy trots along at my side.

We stop at a tiny newsagent's, where a man peers suspiciously from behind a cluttered counter. "Wait here," I tell Daisy at the entrance, digging into my pocket for the pound I stuffed in there and hoping she doesn't run off. The shop guy takes what feels like a million years to give me a small bottle of water and my change, and when I run out of the shop, Daisy is waiting obediently for me.

"Look," I say, "I got you some water." I frown, wondering how she's going to drink it. Where's a handy dog bowl when you need one? I spot a chip carton lying on the ground, tip out the greasy remains – which Daisy gobbles up in an instant – then fill it with water from the bottle. She laps gratefully, as if there wasn't a single drop of water in her body. Then she looks up at me as if to say, "Can I have some more?" Only, that's the whole bottle gone, and nearly all my money, too. I hold her by the collar as we cross the road to a small, oval-shaped patch of grass. As Daisy settles down at my feet, I perch on a bench and try the phone number from her collar tag again.

"Hello?" comes the voice – a real person this time.

"Er . . . hi," I say. "I've got your dog here. I found her, wandering about on her own in the skate park. . ."

"Did you?" the woman exclaims. "Where are you exactly?"

I peer around until I spot a street sign. "Desmond Street . . . we're on a grassy area in front of a flower shop."

"Oh, for goodness' sake," she snaps, as if all of this is *my* fault. I glance down at Daisy and frown. Poor thing. No wonder she ran away if her owner is always this grumpy. "Hang on," the woman adds, before muttering to someone in the background. I grip my phone, prickling with annoyance. Is anything more irritating than a person yakking away to someone else while they're supposed to be having a phone conversation with you? "...Told you about keeping that gate shut," she rants. "Whose idea was it to get this dog anyway? This had better be the last time this happens or she's going back..."

"Hello?" I shout into the phone. She doesn't seem to hear me. She certainly doesn't come back on and say, *Sorry for being so rude. And thank you so much for looking after my overheated, panting dog and buying her a bottle of water.* There are no thanks at all. It's as if she's forgotten I'm here.

"Hi," the woman says finally. "Someone's coming to get her, all right? Won't be long." And she's gone.

"Thanks a lot," I mumble, stuffing my phone back into my pocket and flopping down beside Daisy. The grass is all dried out and not especially soft to lie on, but I don't care. As she snuggles close to me, all the worry and upset of the past week starts to fade away. Maybe because I'm missing Murphy, it feels good being close to a dog again. I don't have to explain myself to her, and she won't start prattling on about my old-fashioned name or what kind of loo we used to have.

The traffic noises are strangely soothing as we lie together. I'm thinking, *Maybe I should call Mum, I'll do it in a minute* ... but I'm so drowsy in the sunshine, I can't muster the energy to pull out my phone. There's the buzz of an insect close to my head, and now I'm drifting, forgetting that I'm on a patch of city grass, surrounded by shops and cars and people. In fact, I'm almost imagining a slight rocking motion, as if I'm lying here not with a big fluffy dog but with Bella and Murphy on Promise's deck. . .

"Daisy! DAISY!"

My eyes ping open. In a flurry of black fur, she jumps up and charges away. I jerk bolt upright, dizzy in the heat. Daisy is running full pelt, ears flapping, towards a dark-haired boy in jeans and a T-shirt. He's standing there with arms outstretched, his face awash with delight. Sending him staggering backwards as she hurls herself at him, Daisy leaps up to cover him with wet doggy kisses.

And . . . I can't say I blame her. He's greeting her as if they've been separated for years. I feel my stomach twist with shyness as I wait for the boy to notice me scrambling up from the ground and trying to brush bits of dried grass off my shorts and bare legs.

"Silly girl, why did you run off?" he asks Daisy, ruffling her fur as she dances around him in delight. Then he stops and looks past her, straight at me. And that smile appears again, as bright and startling as a shooting star.

It's the boy with the bike.

CHAPTER
Twelve

Oh no. Here it comes — that horrible whoosh of self-consciousness, turning me hot pink and incapable of acting like a normal person. "Was it you who phoned?" the boy asks, still all smiles as he saunters towards me, pulling Daisy's red leather lead out of his pocket.

"Yeah," I say with a shrug, like it was nothing.

"Well . . . thanks. Most people wouldn't bother." He blinks at me, and I register his eyes. You couldn't not, really. They're an intense chocolatey brown, framed by the longest lashes I've *ever* seen on a boy.

"Well, I didn't want to leave her wandering about," I say, twisting Bella's ring between my thumb and forefinger. "If she'd left the park, she could have been run over."

The boy nods gratefully, and something like butterflies flit around my heart. "I know. We've only just got her and my little sisters aren't used to having to keep the gate shut yet." He chuckles softly, quickening my heart with another smile. "She's a little escape artist. Trouble is, Mum seems to assume it's me being careless. . ."

"That doesn't sound fair," I suggest.

"Yeah, well." He clips Daisy's lead on to her collar. "Guess that comes with being the oldest."

"How old are you?" I ask.

"Fourteen. That means I'm supposed to be —" he raises a brow "— the responsible one." He laughs, and it's catching; I'm chuckling too, forgetting about feeling awkward and shy. "I'm Leon," he adds, "and you've already met Daisy. Not my choice of name, I might add. My sisters ganged up and won, even though I tried to rig the voting."

"So what would you have called her?" I ask as we sit side by side on the bench while Daisy sprawls at Leon's feet.

"Oh, I dunno — but something less girly, definitely. . . What's your name, anyway?"

"Josie," I tell him, and this time there's no, *What's that short for?*

"Nice name," Leon says, and little seed of shyness starts up in my stomach, quickly swelling as a thought engulfs me: *This is possibly the cutest boy I have ever met. And he saw me in my Dalmatian pyjamas.* Does he even realize I'm the girl who was looking out of her bedroom window at night? Maybe he barely saw me at all. . .

"You live at the Stag, don't you?" Leon says.

Ah. He saw me all right. "Er . . . yes," I reply, my

cheeks flaring up again. "So, um ... what were *you* doing, cycling about in the middle of the night?"

He pushes back his dark fringe. "Er ... it's just something I like doing," he says vaguely.

But why? I want to ask as a shoal of questions flits around in my head. Leon glances at me. He has a few brownish freckles across his nose, and a mouth that constantly looks on the verge of a smile. "So," he says, "how long've you been living at the Stag, then?"

"We only arrived yesterday," I reply.

"Where did you live before?"

I pause, slightly wary of another "Oooh – what happened to your poos and wees?" conversation, which would kind of ruin this moment for me. I decide to risk it. "We used to live on a boat," I say.

"Wow, did you? Where?"

"Well, the nearest village to us, where I went to school, was called Issingworth."

Leon looks blank.

"Better known as the middle of nowhere," I add as Daisy nudges my ankle with her nose.

"She likes you," Leon laughs, glancing down at her. "So ... from a boat to a pub. Why did you move?"

Where on earth do I start? At the beginning, I guess – the day of our party on Promise and Tarragon, when it felt as if the whole summer was spread out in front of us... "And that was that?" Leon asks incredulously when I finally pause for breath.

I nod. "The boatyard man said she was too rotten to be fixed, and we saw for ourselves when she'd been lifted out of the river."

Leon blows out air. "God, that's awful."

I shrug. "Well, it was, but it's happened and Mum says I should look on the bright side. It's kind of hard, though, when I had to leave my best friend *and* my dog behind. . ." My phone trills in my pocket. "Hey, Mum," I say, rolling my eyes at Leon in a *here-we-go* kind of way, even though she's only asking where I am.

"Better go," he mouths, breaking into another heart-melting grin as he gets up from the bench.

"Everything OK, love?" Mum asks. I glance at Leon as he leaves, smiling at the way Daisy keeps looking up at him as she trots at his side.

"Yes, Mum," I say. Right at this moment, as he turns around and waves, life really does seem a little brighter.

CHAPTER
Thirteen

We've lived at the Bald-faced Stag for just five days and already my big brother has landed himself a holiday job.

It's not in the pub, even though he could have talked to Vince and probably picked up a few hours' work clearing tables or washing up ("I'm not spending my summer in that kitchen," he told me with a shudder). Instead, he's found a job with a local gardening company. That's *so* Ryan, happening to spot a shop selling plants and wheelbarrows, with a sign saying "garden maintenance" in the window. He'd marched right in and charmed them. It's decent money, too.

Am I jealous? Not as much as you might think, because now it's often just Mum and me hanging out together. And I'm working, too – Mum says she'll sort out an allowance for me, even though it's unofficial. I'm too young for a proper job, but not to help her around the pub kitchen. We're scrubbing it out right now, from top to bottom, making it a place where she can actually cook. It's hardly the nicest way to spend yet another hot, cloudless day, and occasionally I wonder what Bella's doing – swimming in the lake, or lounging on her deck with her headphones on, immersed in a book? But at least it's keeping me busy, which is handy when there are so many things I *don't* want to think about.

Like, whether Promise has been smashed to bits by now, and if anyone found a scratched blue tin with a home-made book of faded drawings inside. Instead of dwelling on that, I'm on my hands and knees, scrubbing hard at some unidentifiable gunk on the floor.

"This place is disgusting," Mum exclaims, wiping a shirtsleeve across her sweat-dampened forehead. "I feel bad, Josie, you spending your summer holidays doing this."

"It's OK," I say, thinking, *What else could I have done when she came up to the flat for a breather, all smeared with grease and stale cooking smells trapped in her hair?* We start to empty the huge freezer, which obviously hasn't been working properly, because it's full of stinking mush. "Green beans," Mum says, screwing up her face and dropping a sloppy package into the bin bag where all the rotten stuff's going. My next task is to check the use-by dates on the herbs and spices in the big walk-in cupboard. "This one expired before I was born!" I shriek. Into the black bag it goes, and we're giggling now, competing to see who can find the oldest edible thing. "Fifteen-year-old dried parsley," I announce.

"Looks like grey dust – I win!" Mum applauds me, and when Ryan comes home all grubby from trimming hedges, he joins in too. It feels good, all of us mucking in together, making the pub kitchen a bit nicer for Mum.

"When are you putting strawberry tarts on the menu?" I ask, sweeping out some unidentifiable debris from under the huge stainless-steel cooker.

"I think that's way down the line," Mum replies. "There are a few other things I need to broach with Vince and Maria first."

I know what these things are. Everything that comes out of the Stag's kitchen is fried, every plate slicked with yellowy oil. Burgers, sausages, chops, chips – it's hardly the kind of tasty, wholesome food Mum likes to cook. "I'll have to play it carefully," she adds, using a floor brush to sweep away a rogue cobweb on the ceiling that none of us had noticed. "They're proud of this place, and it *is* popular with the local crowd, especially the older ones. I can't march in and change everything all at once." Vince and Maria don't even know about Operation Clean-Up – Mum deliberately waited until they'd gone off to the cash 'n' carry. When Ryan finds a filthy apron stuffed in a cupboard and models it for us, Mum and I are doubled up in hysterics. What Mum finds next is slightly less funny – a mousetrap behind a stack of cooking oil tins, with a dead mouse in it, gone rock-hard. "It's a miracle this place hasn't been shut down by the environmental health people," she exclaims, throwing both trap and mouse into the bin bag and knotting it tightly.

"Are you going to say anything to Vince or Maria?" I ask, giving the floor a final sweep.

"Oh, I don't know." Mum pushes back her hair with a rubber-gloved hand. "They obviously don't care about a bit of filth. . ."

"A *bit*?" I splutter. "It was disgusting, Mum."

"Yes, but you know what?" She smiles wearily. "This job's really important to me – to all of us – and I don't want to upset them or rock the boat. Anyway, it's not really my place to lecture them, is it? They seem like nice, kind people. They're probably just a bit clueless. . ."

"*Are* they?" comes a voice.

The three of us spin round to face the kitchen door. Chantelle is standing there, hand on hip, smirking.

"Oh, I didn't mean it like that," Mum blusters, flushing bright red. "I just mean . . . your mum and dad have probably been under a lot of pressure."

She sniffs and flares her nostrils at us.

"Anyway," Mum croaks, "we had a bit of time to spare, so we thought we'd give the place a quick spruce-up." She swipes a wisp of cobweb from her hair.

Chantelle glances from Mum to me, and finally to Ryan – and there, her expression softens. "Yeah, well," she says in a friendlier voice, "I'm sure they'll be pleased when they see it."

"I hope so." Mum looks around at all of us. "We wouldn't want to offend them, you know."

"I'm sure they won't take it like that, Mrs Lennox," Chantelle replies sweetly.

"Do call me Helen—"

Chantelle nods. "OK. Anyway, I think it's going to be great having you here." With that, she throws Ryan a huge, flirty smile, then turns on her sparkly heeled sandals and clip-clops away.

The three of us gawp at one another in silence, then burst into stifled laughter. "Oooh, Ryan," Mum teases, wrapping an arm around my handsome, dark-eyed brother's shoulders, "seems like you've made quite an impression there."

We're all still sniggering, and I'm mimicking Chantelle's pouty look, when Vince pops his head around the kitchen door. "You lot seem in good spirits today," he remarks with a grin.

"Oh, we are," Mum says, quickly smoothing back her hair and composing herself.

"And you've done a great job with this place." Vince glances around the now-gleaming kitchen, then adds, "Josie – Leon's looking for you. I didn't realize you two had met."

So Vince knows him too. "Oh, we, um . . . we met when I found his dog," I say quickly, conscious of Mum staring at me.

"Well, I said he could come in," Vince says, grinning,

"but he wanted to wait outside."

Now Mum and Ryan are both giving me quizzical looks. "OK, thanks," I say quickly, turning to follow Vince out of the kitchen.

"Hang on," Mum says, grabbing my arm. "Who's Leon?"

I pause, wishing I could just run off, but knowing she'd kick up a fuss. "I just said, Mum. I found his dog wandering about and he came to collect her. We got talking, that's all. . ."

"Got a boyfriend already?" Ryan teases.

"Oh, shut up—"

"I'm not sure I like the idea of you hanging about with someone I don't know," Mum cuts in. "How old is he, anyway?"

"Mum, he's *fine*," I protest. "He's fourteen."

She pulls off one of her rubber gloves with a snap. "OK, but I'm coming outside to meet him first."

What? As she removes the other glove, I'm about to protest that she can't, and that I'm not a baby any more. Then I realize that living in London, and figuring out how to keep us safe – well, it's all new to her, too.

On the river, you see, there were no rules.

CHAPTER
Fourteen

Leon's smile makes me melt like ice cream in the sun. "Hi," he says as I step outside, not looking remotely taken aback that Mum is hovering next to me.

"Hi," I say quickly. "Mum, this is Leon." He's holding Daisy by her lead. I bend to ruffle her fur, hoping that, by the time I straighten up again, Mum will have done her protective parent bit and disappeared back inside.

"Hi, Leon," she says warmly. "Oh, what an adorable dog!"

"Thanks. We only got her a couple of weeks ago."

"Bet she feels like part of the family already," Mum adds, and I wonder if she's thinking about Murphy.

"Yeah, definitely," Leon replies.

"So," Mum says, turning to me, "where are you two thinking of going today?"

"Um . . . we'll probably just hang out at the park," I tell her, while desperately trying to transmit the message that she must go back inside *right now* . . . and that's when I smell something awful.

Oh God. What have I been doing these past two hours? Dealing with dead mice and years' worth of kitchen filth, and the stale smell has attached itself to my clothes and hair. "Er . . . I've been helping Mum clean the kitchen," I say, turning to Leon. "I'd better have a shower first."

Mum laughs. "Good idea, Josie. I didn't like to say." She smiles at Leon. "Would you like to come in and wait in the pub?"

"Er, yes, but. . ." He glances down at Daisy.

"Oh, Vince has gone on some errand," she says, "and there's no one else around right now. I'm sure it'll be fine to bring her in." We all head inside, and I scamper upstairs for the speediest shower known to girl-kind. Afterwards, a thought hits me as I throw on my dressing gown and quickly brush my wet hair. Should I make more of an effort? Should I grab Mum's hairdryer and some of her make-up, too? I might have taken the time to learn to apply it properly if I'd had a mirror on Promise that I could actually see into – but never mind that. Leon's waiting downstairs. I pull on a T-shirt, jeans and a pair of flip-flops and run downstairs, feeling as light as dandelion fluff.

Leon is still there, and Daisy, of course – plus Chantelle. What's she doing, jammed next to Leon on the wooden bench seat in the far corner of the pub? They're so engrossed in each other, they haven't even noticed me. And Chantelle's not terrified of Daisy any more, that's for sure. "I didn't know she was yours when we saw her in the park," she's telling him. "If I had, I'd have brought her straight round to your place. Oh, I'm *so* relieved nothing happened to her. . ."

Leon says something I can't hear while Chantelle pouts and tosses her hair, inches away from his face. She's fully made up in a little lacy top and tiny black skirt, and keeps giggling fakely. Is this how boys like girls to be? Realizing I have absolutely no idea, I look down at my blue and white stripy T-shirt and dark jeans, and at my feet in their flip-flops with unpainted nails. "Oh, I've missed you so much, Leon," she declares, causing my heart to slump. "Now it's the holidays, we've got to spend lots of time together, OK?"

Again, I don't catch Leon's response. But I *do* see that he doesn't exactly shrink away when Chantelle throws her arms around him for a hug. If she's his friend, where am *I* going to fit in? And what if she's more than that . . . an ex-girlfriend, maybe? How awkward would *that* be? After all, I've only just met him, unlike Chantelle, who's obviously closer to him than I could ever hope to be.

Feeling like an idiot for even hoping Leon and I could hang out this summer, I turn around and hurry back upstairs to the flat. Daisy is the only one who even noticed I was there.

CHAPTER
Fifteen

I can't sleep. It's too hot in my room – far hotter than it ever was on Promise. Maybe there was something about living on water that cooled the air, or the fact that she was made from wood allowed our home to breathe.

This room of mine, with its ugly wardrobe and bumpy mustard walls – it doesn't breathe at all.

I sit up, still aware of all the unfamiliar grumbles and creaks of this enormous flat that was once a hotel (there's even a number 3 on my bedroom door. Ryan's is 4, next to me, and Mum's is the one after that). I'm up at my window now, trying to force it open, but it's too stiff.

And that's when I see Leon, looking up at me.

I jump back, wishing I'd never got out of bed. It was awkward enough, explaining to Mum that I'd changed my mind about hanging out with him today (I feigned a stomach ache). When I peer out again, he's still there, giving me a baffled look, as if to say, *What happened?*

I shrug. And then, as he makes no move to go away, I start to feel a bit sheepish. Maybe I shouldn't have stayed in the flat after saying I was only popping upstairs for a shower. And that scene with Chantelle . . . had I misread it in some way? He'd hardly be here now, at just past midnight, if he didn't genuinely want to see me. . .

Gripping his bike with one hand, Leon is beckoning me to come out. I swallow hard, knowing there's no chance of getting to sleep now. I nod, then pull on a thin fleece over my PJ top and swap my pyjama bottoms for jeans. Tiptoeing out into the hall, I grab the keys from the small wooden bowl on the shelf. I unlock the flat door, then creep downstairs, through the dark, stale-smelling pub to the main door, where I manage to slide back two heavy bolts, then unlock the door with the main key.

"Hi," I say shyly as I step outside.

"Hi." Leon fixes me with a quizzical look. "What happened today? Why didn't you come out?"

I blink at him, not caring that my hair is probably sticking up in bed-head tufts. "Er . . . I changed my mind," I reply quietly. "I didn't feel too good."

"I tried to find your mum to ask her, but I think she was busy in the kitchen." He pauses, pushing back his dark hair distractedly. "She really wanted to check me out, didn't she?"

I shrug. "Yeah, I guess she did."

He smiles, his brown eyes glinting in the silvery light

from the street lamp. "It's nice that she's protective like that."

"You think so?"

"Yeah. At least she cares."

"Why," I start, "doesn't your mum—"

"Look, Josie," he cuts in, "has Chantelle been giving you a hard time?"

I pause, wondering how to put it, seeing as they seem so . . . *close*. "She's not exactly friendly," I say, hoping it sounds as if I don't care. "It's OK, though. I can handle it."

He bites his lip, as if trying to figure out the best way to explain things. "The trouble with Chantelle is. . ." he starts.

"What d'you mean, the *trouble*?" I ask with a small laugh. "You're friends, aren't you?"

"We're, um. . ." He pauses. "Look, I've known her for a long time – long enough to know that she's used to getting what she wants." He tails off with a smirk.

"Right," I say, having to stop myself from firing more questions.

He climbs on to his bike, standing astride it without making any move to cycle away. "D'you, um . . . still want to hang out sometime?"

I wonder what Chantelle would make of that, and quickly push the thought away. "Yeah, sure."

"Can I have your number?"

I've lived here for less than a week and already, the

cutest boy I've ever set eyes on wants to call me. As I tell him my number and he taps it into his phone, a light goes on in the flat above. "Someone's in the bathroom," I say quickly. "I'd better get back inside."

"See you soon, then," he says, and I'm on the verge of asking, *Why are you out at night? Does nobody care about you?* But too late – he's gone.

CHAPTER

Sixteen

"Say hello, Murphy! Say hi to Josie. . ." It's 8.30 a.m., and Bella has called my mobile, bringing a blast of sunshine into my mustard bedroom.

"Hi, Murphy," I croak, still in bed as I grip my phone.

"Aw, he won't bark," Bella says. "He's wagging his tail, though. Want to talk to him?"

"Go on then," I snigger, "put him on." After a brief, one-sided conversation, Bella comes back on the phone.

"It's not the same without you," she declares. "All the boaters keep asking if I've heard from you and how you're getting on."

"Really?"

"Of course they do! D'you think they'd have forgotten you already?" Although I'm smiling, I'm aware of a tug of longing for my old life. "Maggie and Phil were asking about you too," Bella continues. "In fact, they seemed a bit confused about something and wanted me to mention it to you. . ."

"What is it?"

"Well," she says, "they needed to have work done on Mucky Duck's engine, so they took her to that boatyard you went to. When they came back to pick her up a couple of days later, they noticed a boat in the yard that looked just like Promise."

"Really?" I exclaim.

"Yeah! Same shaped hull, same narrow windows – same everything, really."

"That's *so* weird." I frown, propping up my pillows against the bumpy wall so I can sit up more comfortably. "It couldn't have been Promise, though. She was being taken away to the scrapyard because Bill needed the space."

"That's what I told them," Bella says. "Maggie said this boat had a different name anyway – Lily-May. And when she asked Bill about her, he said she was some old heap he'd been working on for years, and that he was putting her up for sale."

I bite my lip, trying to shrug off a creeping sense of unease. "Were they sure it was the same kind of boat as ours?"

"I asked them that," Bella says. "Phil said they were *dead* sure – they were absolutely convinced."

"Well, they did live opposite us since I was little. I suppose they'd know, probably better than anyone else. It's strange, though. Mum's always wondered if there were any more boats still around, built from her granddad's plans. And I guess there must be. . ."

"D'you think that boat could actually be Promise?" Bella asks cautiously.

"I don't see how she could be. She was rotten, we saw that for ourselves. And anyway, you said this boat was called . . . what was it again?"

"Lily-May." Bella pauses, and I know exactly what she's thinking.

"A boat's name can be changed, of course. It's as simple as painting it over. . ."

"Bad luck, though," she adds.

"For who?" I ask. "The person who did it?"

"I guess so, yeah."

We fall silent for a moment. "Bella," I start, "this doesn't seem right, does it? It's too coincidental. Maybe that boat *was* Promise, and Bill was lying. . ."

". . .And perhaps she was fixable after all," she cuts in. "God, Josie. What are you going to do?"

"I don't know," I whisper as too many questions fly around my head: were Maggie and Phil mistaken? And if they weren't, and Lily-May really is our boat, how could we go about getting her back?

"The must be some way you could prove it," Bella adds.

"Yes . . . I know."

Mum is calling me now, saying, "Breakfast's ready, Josie, hurry up unless you want rubbery scrambled eggs. . ."

"Your tin!" Bella exclaims, as if reading my thoughts. "Your tin should still be there under your bed."

*

I can hardly eat breakfast for replaying Bella's phone call in my head. Luckily, Mum is too busy scribbling to-do lists at the kitchen table to notice and, after shovelling in his eggs at breakneck speed, Ryan rushes off to work.

Shall I tell Mum about the boat Maggie and Phil saw? She looks engrossed in work, trying to figure out the supplies she'll need for the next few days. Anyway, I know she'd say it's just wishful thinking that Lily-May might have been Promise after all. "Mum," I say hesitantly, placing my fork beside my barely touched breakfast, "d'you think Bill will have had Promise taken away by now?"

She glances up at me and frowns. "Why aren't you eating, Josie? You don't still feel ill, do you?"

"No, I'm fine. So what d'you think? About Promise, I mean?"

"I don't know. Yes, probably." With a sigh, she turns back to her list. I snatch my phone from my pocket as it bleeps, assuming it's Bella again, maybe with more info from Maggie and Phil.

The text reads: *Hi, it's Leon. U coming out?*

My mouth curls into a grin. *Sure*, I reply, pushing away my plate. *When?*

Now? Leon pings back. *Am outside.*

I bite my lip, glancing at Mum while trying to appear as calm as possible. "Er . . . is it OK if I go out?" I ask casually.

"Who with, love?" Mum's frowning, still scribbling away with a cracked biro.

"Just Leon."

"*Just* Leon, huh?" She looks up, her eyes crinkling as she laughs. "He's bright and early, isn't he?"

"Yeah, guess so." I shrug and take a swig of my juice, as if being texted by a boy at breakfast time is completely normal for me.

"That's fine," Mum says, "but remember to take your phone, all right? And let me know where you are."

"OK, thanks, Mum," I say, forgetting about my oh-so-casual act as I leap up from the table, nearly knocking over my glass of juice. Pretending I haven't heard her as she calls after me, telling me to at least eat something first, I charge out of the kitchen and head downstairs. By the time I'm pulling back the bolts on the pub's heavy front door, I've already decided not to mention Chantelle today. So what if she and Leon are friends? I barely know either of them, really. Even so, Leon's dark eyes make my heart flip as I step out into the faint drizzle.

"I wondered if you'd be up," he says.

"I can't lie in here," I explain. "S'pose I'm still not used to all the traffic noise. . ." I sense myself blushing. How dumb that sounds, as if Promise was moored on some distant, people-less planet.

"You'll stop hearing it after a while," he says with a smile. "Anyway, fancy coming over to my place today? We can hang out in the summer house if you like."

"A summer house?" I exclaim. Now it's Leon's turn to look embarrassed.

"Oh, it's nothing," he says quickly as we head along Castle Street. "Just an old shed really. You'll see." I'm intrigued now, my curiosity growing as the dingy streets soon make way for bigger houses, then huge posh ones, their gardens hidden behind ivy-covered walls with elaborate iron gates. It's raining harder now, and we hurry along, not saying much. These houses have names instead of numbers – like "The Nook" and "BriarVilla". Leon's place, which sits proudly at the end of a curving gravelled drive, is called The Willows. The enormous garden is neat at first, with bright yellow flowers edging each side of the drive. But it soon turns into a tangle of weeds as we make our way to a cream-coloured wooden building at the bottom.

"Is that your summer house?" I ask.

He nods. "Told you it was just a shed."

"No it's not," I retort. "It's *beautiful*." I stop for a moment, taking in the arched windows, the blue pointed roof and the pots of red flowers outside. Sure, the paintwork is flaking, and now we're closer I can see that the roof's sagging a bit. But it's still incredibly pretty and peaceful, like something out of a fairy tale. Down here, you can hardly hear traffic at all.

"Come in," Leon says, pushing the door open. I follow him inside, breathing in the warm, woody scent of the place. It's actually a bit like being inside Promise.

"You're so lucky," I exclaim, glancing down at the brightly patterned floor cushions strewn around, and the assortment of maps and postcards pinned up in-between the windows.

"I guess it depends on what you mean by lucky," he says.

"I mean having a summer house all of your own."

"Yeah, well, it's on the verge of collapse. Dad's planning to take it down sometime this year—"

"No," I say. "He can't do that!"

Leon shrugs as we settle on the biggest, squashiest cushions. "It's been neglected, sadly. My parents have been too busy building up their business to pay much attention to this place. . ."

"What kind of business do they have?" I ask.

"They import stuff from all over the world – ornaments, bowls and rugs and all sorts, from places like India. Then they sell them at vastly inflated prices. Clever, huh?" He laughs dryly.

"Um . . . I guess so."

"So they've kind of left me and my sisters to our own devices," Leon continues. He grabs a cloth from the table and mops up a splosh of rainwater beside it. "See what I mean about the state of this place? Anyway," he adds, "tell me more about your boat."

I pause, realizing there's so much I'm bursting to share, I don't know where to begin. But once I've started, it all pours out: about Maggie and Phil spotting Lily-May at

Bill's boatyard, and the tin I'd stashed under my bed. Of course, this means I have to explain about Dad dying, too. "That's terrible," he says. "It must've been awful for you."

I nod, unable to speak for a moment. I'm not used to talking about Dad, that's the problem. When we lived on the river, everyone knew, so there was no need to explain things. "It was a long time ago," I say softly.

"So . . . what kind of things did you have in your tin?"

"Mainly newspaper cuttings. Dad was a cross-country running champion and there were articles about that. There were a couple of photos of him as a little boy, and this thing he made, a book of drawings of the seven wonders of the ancient world. . ." I stop abruptly, realizing only Bella knows this part. "I've only ever told my best friend about that," I add, feeling suddenly shy.

"You didn't even tell your mum?" he asks gently.

I shake my head. "At first, when I was younger, I just wanted something secret of my own – the way little kids do, you know?" Leon nods, encouraging me to go on. "Especially living on a boat, where there's hardly any space and *nothing's* private. Anyway, I knew it would probably upset Mum if she found out I had this personal collection of Dad's things. And then. . ."

". . .Then what?" Leon says.

"It seemed. . ." I gnaw at a fingernail. "So much time

had gone by, it seemed too late to tell her. I mean, what would I have said – 'Er, Mum, here's a tin of Dad's stuff that I've kept all these years'?"

"I see what you mean," he says. We fall into silence, broken only by the soft patter of rain on the summer-house roof. "So," he says, jumping up from his cushion, "what about these wonders of the world? Can you name them all?"

"Of course I can," I say, laughing. I mean, how many times have I looked through Dad's little book?

"Go on then," he says with a grin, indicating a map on the wall.

"Um. . ."As I scan the brightly coloured countries, the only wonder that comes to mind is Leon's insanely long eyelashes, which perfectly frame those melting brown eyes. "Er . . . the pyramids," I mutter finally, feeling my cheeks glowing pink. He takes a coloured pin from a jar on the table and sticks it on to Egypt.

"OK . . . and the next one?" he asks in a teasing voice.

I bite my lip. "The Hanging Gardens of Babylon," I blurt out, expecting him to not have a clue where to stick a pin this time, but he does. It goes into what's now Iraq.

"I thought you'd just be able to rattle them off straight away," he teases.

I laugh and shake my head. "My mind's gone completely blank."

"Well," he says, "what about the Lighthouse of

Alexandria, the Mausoleum at Halicarnassus … the Statue of Zeus at Olympia. . ."

"How d'you know them?" I exclaim.

He grins. "In seven years of being home-educated, it's about the *only* thing I learnt."

"You mean you don't go to school?" I ask incredulously.

"Yep, that's right."

"So . . . who teaches you? Your mum and dad?"

Leon shrugs. "In theory, yeah. At least, they started off with good intentions. But then, as they had more and more kids – there are four of us – the novelty wore off. . ."

"So none of you have been to school at all?" I ask.

"Oh, I did a few years of primary."

"Is that allowed, though? I thought school was compulsory."

"Well, it is," he says, "but anyone can home-educate their kids if they want to."

"But. . ." I pause, wondering if I'm firing too many questions. "I thought there were checks and stuff, to make sure kids are learning."

He shakes his head. "Amazingly, no. Or maybe we've been forgotten about. Anyway, it's pretty good, having loads of freedom. . ."

My heart turns over as his eyes meet mine. "Is that why you go out at night? Just because you can?"

He laughs softly. "I guess so. This might sound mad, but it's also pretty much the only time I get some space to myself. You see, being the oldest, a lot of the home-educating has kind of fallen to me."

I'm digesting this – the fact that a fourteen-year-old boy has found himself teaching his sisters – when there's a burst of high-pitched yelling outside, followed by the scrunch of feet on wet gravel. "Talking of which," Leon adds as the shouting reaches fever pitch, "block your ears, Josie. Here they come."

CHAPTER
Seventeen

The summer-house door crashes open as three rain-dampened girls tumble in.

"Hey, *we're* hanging out in here today," Leon protests.

"But it's raining," declares the smallest one. She turns to me with a gap-toothed grin. "Hi," she says boldly.

"Hi," I reply, overwhelmed by these wet-haired girls who have stopped their babbling and all turned to stare at me.

"This is Josie," Leon says, and I can see now that he's a good head taller than the eldest of his sisters. "Her family's just moved into the Stag. Her mum's the new chef there."

"Oh!" the little one exclaims, giving her big brother a significant, wide-eyed look. "That's Chantelle's mum and dad's pub."

"Yeah," Leon replies. "Yeah ... it is." I know I'm being stupid, wincing at the mention of Chantelle's name, but I can't help it. "This is Rosie," Leon adds, indicating the smallest girl. "So-called not 'cause she's sweet-smelling or anything, but because she's a thorn in my side." He goes to play-punch her and she dissolves into giggles, dispelling the brief sense of unease that filled the summer house.

"Hi, Rosie," I say.

"Hi, Josie," Rosie splutters, highly amused by our rhyming names.

"Next up," Leon says, "is Lexi. . ."

A girl with fluffy short hair pops her chewing gum. "Hi, Josie!"

"Hello, Lexi. . ."

"And this is Beth." As Leon introduces her, the tallest sister tosses back a thick fringe.

"Hiya," she says with a huge smile.

"Nice to meet you all," I say, wondering what we'll do now, as it's pretty crowded with five of us in the summer house. I brush away a twinge of disappointment as the three girls sprawl on to the scattered cushions, making no move to leave.

"So," Rosie says, grinning up at me, "are you Leon's girlfriend or what?"

"Excuse me," he cuts in quickly while my cheeks burn red hot. "Since when was my life any of your business?"

"I only asked," she says smugly while her older sisters snigger away.

"Yeah, well," Leon says gruffly, "like I said, we're

hanging out in here today. I know you wanted to check Josie out, and now you have – so bye-bye."

"Aw, Leon, you're *so* mean." Rosie fixes her big brother with a wide-eyed look, her skinny light-brown plaits hanging like damp tails at her shoulders. The way he acts with his sisters – impatient, but kind enough to not send them packing right away – is making me warm to him even more. "But what does Chantelle think about—" Rosie starts, at which Leon's expression darkens immediately.

"Rosie – shut *up*," he barks, turning to me and rolling his eyes. "Anyway, it's stopped raining now, OK? Go find something else to do."

While Beth and Lexi gather themselves up and head outside, Rosie stays put. "Please, Leon," she says. "Let me stay. Let's . . . um. . ." He throws me a quick apologetic look. "Let's play dares!" she announces.

He sighs loudly. "OK. I dare you to get out of here and leave us in peace."

"No!"

Well, that's what I want too, of course. I want it to be just the two of us, and I also want to ask why Rosie mentioned Chantelle in that way, as if she knows it winds him up. But how would I do that without sounding jealous? I haven't a clue how to *be* with him, that's the problem. Leon has burst into my life with his incredible smile, like no one I've ever met before. As he and Rosie chatter away, my gaze skims the seven pins he's stuck in the map, each one correctly placed.

"What d'you think, Josie?" Leon cuts into my thoughts.

"Sorry?" I snap back to the present.

"The dare. D'you reckon she'll do it?"

"Oh, I think so," I bluff as Rosie, who clearly adores her brother, giggles at his side. Then she clatters out of the summer house, and we stand watching in the doorway as she scampers across the wet lawn towards the imposing stone house. "Er . . . what did you dare her to do again?" I ask.

He grins, those intense brown eyes meeting mine and making my stomach swirl. "You're funny. You were daydreaming there, weren't you?" *No, I was thinking how horribly unfair it would be if, when I've only just met you, it turns out you already belong to someone else. . .*

"Yeah," I say, sensing my cheeks reddening.

"Well, I dared her to fetch her trumpet from her bedroom, then balance on the garden wall and blast out twenty-five notes."

"Oh, right." I laugh as Rosie reappears, waving a gleaming gold instrument above her head. As she clambers up on to the crumbly old wall, I find myself holding my breath. "What if she falls?" I gasp.

"She won't. She's like a little monkey."

I chuckle as Rosie teeters on the wall, her face a huge, sunny grin as she beams at us. The rain has stopped now, and the sun peeps out from behind thin, pale clouds as

I glance at Leon. Here in this huge, leafy garden, I feel a million miles from the Stag and my gloomy mustard bedroom. After the rain, everything looks bright and fresh as Rosie puts the trumpet to her lips and starts to blow. We both burst out laughing as her first note fills the air, sounding like a squawking duck.

"What's going on out here?" A sharp female voice comes from the house.

Rosie stops dead and scrambles down the wall, bashing her trumpet against it as she leaps on to the damp, springy grass. "Nothing, Mummy," she says, bold as anything.

I glance at Leon as he raises an eyebrow at me. "Mum," he whispers.

"Had I better go?" I murmur.

"Just hang on a minute. . ."

I can see her now – a tall, skinny woman in a grey dress, her hair cut in a sharp bob and swinging around her pale, pointed face. Daisy is standing meekly at her side. "It didn't look like nothing to me," she snaps, her harsh voice at odds with the sweet-scented day. "You were up on the wall, Rosie, I saw you. What are you playing at?"

"My trumpet," she replies.

"Yes, but what were you doing on the wall with it?"

"Practising," she says simply.

The woman shakes her head, frowning as she glances in our direction. She gives me a quizzical look, as if to say, *And who the hell are you?*, before turning back to Rosie again. "Don't be cheeky."

"But you said I should practise more," Rosie says, and I feel a giggle start somewhere deep in my belly.

"Just go inside and put your trumpet away," her mum says coolly, at which Rosie scampers towards the rickety-looking porch at the back of the house. "And Leon," she adds, not even acknowledging that I'm standing beside him, "I need you to come in and help with some orders. *Now.*"

She frowns at him, and he gives me a quick, apologetic look. "I will, Mum, but it's just . . . I've got a friend here. This is Josie, she's the one who found Daisy—"

"Oh, did you?" she says, blinking at me. "Thank you." She turns away from us, and Leon's cheeks flush and he looks down at the ground.

"Sorry about this," he mutters under his breath.

"It's OK," I whisper, "but I think I'd better go. . ."

Leon nods. "D'you remember the way home?"

"Yeah, sure. It's easy." I can feel his mum giving me a sharp look as I hurry away, past the clumps of cheerful yellow flowers, towards the gates.

"Josie, hang on!"

I whirl round to see Leon running after me. "Wait a minute," he says, catching his breath. "I wanted to say something in the summer house. About that boat. . ."

"What d'you mean?" I start.

"You know, the one those people saw that looked just

like Promise . . . aren't you going to find out for sure?"

I frown at him. "How would I do that?"

Leon pushes back dishevelled dark hair. "How about phoning the boatyard guy and pretending to be interested in buying her?"

"I couldn't do that," I exclaim. "I'd never be able to pull it off."

"Why not? It's only a phone call."

I shake my head firmly. "No, Leon. He'd be bound to know."

"Oh, come on," he teases, grabbing my arm. "I dare you. What have you got to lose? Just call him and find out what's going on."

CHAPTER
Eighteen

As I speed-walk home, I think about Rosie with her trumpet, balancing on a wall that's about twice my height. If a five-year-old is brave enough to do that, *and* to stand up to her scary mum, then surely I can muster the courage to make a quick call to Bill's boatyard. I turn into Castle Street, noticing that the flowers in the pub's window boxes look even sadder than they did this morning, even though they've been rained on. As I approach the pub, sidestepping litter and a scattering of yellowy rice, I rehearse the conversation I might have with Bill.

Er . . . hello, Mr McIntyre. I hear you have a boat, Lily-May, for sale. Could I just ask if she's had a recent name change. . .? No, that wouldn't do.

Hello, Bill. I heard you were sending a friend's boat to the scrapyard. I don't suppose you still have her, do you? It's just. . . Just what, exactly? I'm useless at this. I'm going to fail at Leon's dare, without even trying.

I march into the pub, which is still half-full from the lunch-time crowd. Some of the regulars recognize me now, and give me a smile and a "Hi, love" as I pass. Vince winks at me from behind the bar as he pours a pint, and I glimpse Mum darting about through the frosted-glass kitchen door. Good – she's busy. And as Ryan will still be at work, I'll have the flat to myself. I poke my head into the kitchen, waving to Mum as she and Maria set out slices of apple pie. "Have a nice time, love?" Mum asks distractedly.

"Yes, thanks." I turn and scamper upstairs, my head filled with Leon's words to me.

I dare you. What have you got to lose?

In my room, I lie on my lumpy bed, wondering what to do next. I can't mention any of this to Mum, at least not yet. She's run off her feet most of the time (there are obviously not enough staff here. Maybe that's why the previous chef walked out?). Anyway, if I start on about Promise again she'll get annoyed, and assume I can't accept that we're living in London for good. After all, I did agree to try and make the best of things here.

From down in the street comes a burst of screechy laughter. I jump up off my bed and peer out to see Chantelle, her friend Gemma and a whole bunch of other girls who I don't know, all clattering along in a big clump. In just three weeks, I'll be going to school with them. Mum has been on to the council and arranged for me and Ryan to start at Luffenden Grove, a huge modern block splattered in bird poo where Chantelle and Gemma go. "It's a lively school," I heard Vince telling Mum, "but they'll both be fine there. I'll ask Chantelle to take Josie under her wing." Yeah, right. That makes it feel a *lot* less daunting...

In fact, when I think about school, the whole Promise business seems even more urgent. OK, I might be getting all excited about nothing. After all, Maggie and Phil just saw a boat that *looked* like ours. But what if it really was Promise? That would mean Bill had lied, and that the rotten bits could be replaced after all. And say he'd had her repaired, then decided to sell her ... what then? Would she legally still belong to us? If she did, maybe we could leave this miserable flat and go back to the river, *and* our old school, and have Bella next door...

With my head whirling with possibilities, I grab my phone and call Leon. "Are you busy right now?" I blurt out.

"No, I was helping Mum to pack up some orders but I've finished now. Why ... is everything OK?"

He sounds so concerned, I immediately feel less alone. "Um ... could you find a phone number for me? I'd do it myself but we don't have a computer yet."

"Sure," he says. "Who's it for?"

"Bill McIntyre's boatyard in Clingford."

"You're going to do it!" he exclaims.

I can't help smiling. "Yeah. Well, you dared me, didn't you?"

"Yes, but I didn't think—"

"Have you found the number yet?" I cut in.

Leon laughs. "Give me a minute, will you? I'll get my laptop and text it to you. What's the place called again?"

"Something like McIntyre Boat Repair and Maintenance."

"I'll find it." Less than two minutes later, my phone pings with a text: *01632 171234. Lx*

Lx! Not that I'm reading too much into that. Anyway, more importantly, I have the number. . .

I bite my lip, aware of terrible thumping rock music drifting up from the pub jukebox downstairs. Of course, this might come to nothing. Even if it was Promise that Maggie and Phil saw at the yard, it doesn't mean she's still there. My heart is thumping as I tap out the number on my mobile.

"Hello?" The blunt male voice throws me, as it's obviously someone much younger than Bill.

"Er . . . hello." I clear my throat awkwardly. What had I planned to say again? "Ummm . . . I'm just calling to find out about a boat you have for sale," I say in a weird, robotic voice.

"Which one?" the man asks.

"Erm. . ." Now my tongue feels as if it's stuck to the

roof of my mouth. "It's a wooden boat called. . ." Oh no! What was her name again? Lily-something. My mind has gone blank. I wish Bella was here, giving me courage. "She's very old," I babble, "and has three cabins and. . ."

"Oh, yeah?" he says, sounding as if he is barely listening now.

"Has she been sold?" I croak.

"Hmm. . ." the man mutters. My heart is thumping so loudly, it's a wonder he can't hear it. "Hang on," he adds. "Yeah, I think she's still here."

She's still there! "So . . . is she still for sale?" I ask.

No reply.

"Hello?" I say loudly.

There's a shuffling noise, then some mumbling I can't decipher. "Here's my dad," the man says finally. "You can ask him."

My jaw clenches as he says something else to a man in the background. It's all muffled, as if he's put a hand over the phone. Then an older man — presumably Bill — barks into the phone. "You're calling about Lily-May?"

"Yes," I say brightly, hoping I sound much older than a thirteen-year-old girl.

"Well, we've had a lot of interest," he drawls. "In fact, someone's coming over this afternoon to have a look at her."

"Oh, but I'm *really* interested," I butt in. "If you can

hold on for a day or two. . ." What am I saying? Going to the yard to check out this boat would have to involve Mum. That is, if she'd even agree to take time off work to come with me.

"I can't hang around," he says sharply. "If a buyer comes along, the boat's sold – simple as that. I'm running a business here, not a charity."

"No, I understand," I say meekly.

"Well," he adds, "if you want to view her you'd better be quick. You'll find all the details on my website." With that, he finishes the call.

"Thanks a lot," I growl, placing my phone on my bedside table. I'm about to call Bella when Mum's face, all flushed from the heat of the kitchen, appears around my bedroom door.

"That's the main lunch-time rush over," she says. "I don't suppose you've made yourself a sandwich or anything, have you?"

I shake my head.

"Come on, sweetheart. There's a bit of veggie lasagne left if you fancy it. Believe it or not, it went down really well with the regular crowd today."

"Thanks, Mum," I say, following her to the kitchen. She's a fantastic cook, and I'm glad she's managing to improve the menu, having replaced the horrible frozen burgers with her home-made meals. Even so, I still can't accept that this place will ever feel like our real home.

Later, as Ryan enthuses about his job, and how his boss described him as "a real worker", I still feel miles away. "Everything all right, Josie?" Mum asks as we settle down to watch TV in the living room.

"I'm fine, Mum," I say firmly, glancing around at the ugliest wallpaper I've ever seen. The pattern is of rust-coloured flowers over a pale lemon background. Who in their right mind would choose that?

She catches my eye. "I'm going to have a word with Vince and Maria to see if they'd be OK about us redecorating. We need to cheer the place up a bit." I nod and glance at the quiz show on TV. "You'd both help, wouldn't you?" she asks hopefully.

"Yeah, course," Ryan replies.

"Josie?" Mum prompts me.

"Er . . . yeah." I peer down at my fingernails.

She frowns, exasperated. "You seem as if you're miles away tonight. I'd just like to make the place feel like ours, you know?"

"Yes, I know," I reply. "Erm . . . I'm just a bit tired tonight, Mum. Think I'll have an early night." Although I arrange my expression in a fake, perky smile, she still fixes me with worried eyes as I leave the room.

In the privacy of my bedroom, I text Leon again: *Can I come over tomorrow? Need to check something on laptop.* Then I sit and wait. Maybe one day, we'll get around to buying a computer like every other person in the civilized world, and then I won't have to keep asking favours. On the plus side, though, it's an excuse to spend more time at Leon's.

My phone pings. *No prob*, he replies, and there it is again – *Lx*. Which makes me smile a *real* smile this time.

CHAPTER
Nineteen

There are no sisters around the next day. It's just me and Leon in the summer house, and he's already found Lily-May on Bill McIntyre's website.

For sale
A rare opportunity to acquire a unique
vintage houseboat for relaxed cruising
or living (ideal for family of four)

* Wooden construction throughout, recently restored to the highest standard
* Original interior in excellent condition
* Smooth-running GL12 engine

Must be seen to be fully appreciated
Price £75,000

We both stare at the photo of the boat moored against a narrow wooden jetty. "It looks like Promise," I breathe. "The only difference is her name, but then, anyone could have stripped it off, revarnished the wood and painted on a new one."

Leon nods and looks at me. "Look how much he's selling her for."

"I know. It's unbelievable." I turn and glance through the summer-house's window that overlooks the garden. The droopy branches of a huge weeping willow are swaying in the breeze, and there's a burst of laughter from up by the house. I cross my fingers that Leon's sisters won't all storm in.

"What are you going to do?" he asks.

I exhale loudly. "I don't know. I suppose I hadn't thought things through that far. But I guess the only way to find out if she's really our boat is to go there and see for myself."

Leon frowns. "With your mum?"

I sit back on a stripy floor cushion. "I . . . don't want to tell her, Leon. I don't want to say anything until I know for sure."

He throws me a confused look. "Why not?"

"She'll be annoyed that I've got involved at all, and anyway, what if she says we *can't* go? What would I do then?"

Leon sits on the cushion beside me, causing a shiver to run through me as his bare arm brushes against mine. "I see what you mean. Maybe *you* should go, then."

"That's what I was thinking," I murmur, realizing that that's exactly what I have to do.

"And if your tin's still there, you'll know for certain. . ."

I nod, flinching as a flash of pink appears in the garden. It's Rosie, charging across the uncut lawn. Thankfully, she doesn't even glance at the summer house.

"Do boats have serial numbers?" Leon asks.

"There probably is a number on the engine or something," I say, "but Mum won't have kept a note of it. She's never been organized like that." We slip into a thoughtful silence that doesn't feel remotely awkward.

"Josie," Leon says finally, "if you're going to the boatyard, I want to come with you."

I look at him, amazed. "Why?"

"Because. . ." He shrugs and grins sheepishly. "I just do. It'll be fun."

"But how would you get away with it? Wouldn't your parents think it was weird if you were missing for a whole day?"

Leon laughs, and I realize how dumb I'm being. "They won't even notice. I've been doing my midnight bike rides for a few months now and they've never suspected anything. I think I'll be able to disappear for a few hours without them calling the police."

I'm trying to keep down my smile as I glance at the coloured pins on his map, where he marked out

127

the seven wonders of the world. "Are you sure?" I ask, turning back to him.

"Totally. So how would we get there?"

"We'd have to take a train, then a bus. . ."

"Sounds OK. What would you tell your mum?"

I pause. "Um . . . I don't know, but I'm sure I'll think of something."

His eyes seem to bore into mine. "She won't go mad, will she? When she finds out, I mean."

"Not if it really *is* Promise," I say firmly. "How could she, if it proves that Bill was lying to us all along?"

"If you're sure it'll be OK," he says with a smile.

"Yeah, of course I am. We lost our home, and maybe we needn't have after all. Mum will be so happy when she finds out the truth."

For that moment, in the wood-scented warmth of the summer house, if feels as if nothing could possibly go wrong.

"So you think I'm doing the right thing?" I whisper late that night, after Bella has filled in me in on everything Murphy's done these past few days.

"Course I do," she says. "It's the only way you're going to find out for certain."

From my sitting-up position in bed, I fix my gaze on the muddy-coloured night sky. At nearly eleven p.m., there's still not a star out there. "You don't think it's a mad thing to do?"

"Well, yes," she laughs warmly, "but I know you can pull it off. Or rather, you and Leon can. . ." The smile spreads across my face. "So," she adds, "aren't you going to tell me more about him?"

Where do I start? By describing his melting brown eyes and his lightly tanned skin that just seems to say "summer". I describe his smile, and the way it not only lights up his face, but somehow makes me believe that everything's going to be all right.

"Can't wait to meet him," Bella says.

"Hopefully you will soon." I pause before adding, "Is it OK if I pretend I'm coming to see you on the day we go to the boatyard?"

"It's fine," she says firmly. "But how will you say you're getting here?"

"Er. . ." I chew at a fingernail. "I thought maybe I could tell Mum your dad's picking me up." I shift position in bed, aware of a niggle of guilt in the pit of my stomach.

"That's a good idea," Bella agrees. "Your mum knows he comes to London quite often to do jobs and pick up supplies."

I swallow hard. "You won't say a word to anyone about this, will you?"

"No, of course not."

"Great. Well, I'll figure out the details so Mum doesn't suspect anything. It just seems. . ." I tail off, trying to figure out the best way to explain it. "It feels important that no one else knows about this right now. No one apart from you, that is."

"Or Leon," she adds, and I know she's grinning.

"Yeah." There's a moment of silence, and it feels good, knowing she's there.

"He sounds lovely," she adds with a sigh. "Sometimes, you know, I think maybe it wouldn't be so bad to move away from the river and *do* stuff, meet new people. . ."

"I didn't have any choice, though, did I?" I say gently.

"Yeah, I know that. It's just . . . I keep thinking, Josie's in London, how exciting is that? And you've already met this amazing boy. . ."

"He's just a friend," I remind her, pushing away the image that pops into my mind occasionally – of Chantelle throwing her arms around him in the pub. Which I've convinced myself didn't mean a thing, because he'd hardly be spending time with me if there was still something going on between them, would he?

"Yeah, at the moment," Bella teases. "But who knows what'll happen when the two of you set off on your big trip together? God, it's exciting. You're so lucky."

Me . . . *lucky*? Hardly. But later, as Bella and I say goodnight, I wonder if I am, just a little bit.

CHAPTER
Twenty

I'm perched on a stool in our kitchen, watching Mum make a cake. Actually, I've been pretending to read a book, but I keep glancing over as she lifts each of the three cake layers off their wire cooling trays and starts to sandwich them on top of each other with raspberry jam.

They're stacked high – like the lies I'm telling her now.

"So," I say, trying to sound casual, "Bella's asked me over for the day. Charlie's coming to London anyway, so he can pick me up."

Mum glances at me and frowns. "Really? That's a long way for him to come."

"Not really," I continue, sensing my cheeks starting to glow. "He comes here quite a lot, Mum."

"Yes, I know, but—"

"And he's got to pick up some, er ... special equipment for a job, and then he'll have to return it. So he'll be able to bring me home too." I take a big swig of orange juice in an attempt to cool myself down.

"Oh." Mum pulls a thoughtful face. "That's very kind of him."

"Yes, it is." I smile quickly and try to focus on my book, although the words aren't making much sense. In fact, last night, when I planned all this with Bella, I hadn't imagined how guilty I'd feel. It might be different if my mum was like Leon's, who'd barely looked at me the other day as she'd grudgingly thanked me for finding Daisy. Then it might feel OK to tell a small ... well, maybe not *quite* so small fib. But my mum is nothing like Leon's. She's kind and thoughtful, and would do anything for Ryan and me. After all, that's why she's working all hours in the pub kitchen — it's for us.

"Well, it'll be nice for you to have a day with Bella," she says, spreading sweet, creamy topping over her cake. "As long as you're sure it's OK for Charlie to ferry you back and forth."

"Of course it is," I say, glancing at her finished creation. A layer cake.

Liar cake, more like, says a little voice in my head.

"I know you miss her," Mum continues, "and you've been so good about moving here." I smile stiffly. "So, when are you going?" she asks, studding the topping with glacé cherries.

"Er ... the day after tomorrow, about ten-ish, I think."

Mum nods. "It'll be nice to see Charlie. If I'm

working, make sure he pops into the pub kitchen to say hi, won't you?"

"Yeah, sure," I say brightly.

Mum smiles broadly. "I'm glad you've given me a bit of notice, sweetheart. Remember how much Bella loved those strawberry tarts I made for our last party on *Promise*?"

"Um, yeah. . ." Oh no. I know what's coming next.

"I'll make a big batch for you to take with you," she continues. "I know they're a bit fragile and not the easiest things to transport, but I'm sure you'll manage."

Mum fixes me with her pale blue eyes. I feel so bad, it's a miracle she can't *smell* the guilt radiating off me.

"Think a dozen will be enough to share out with everyone?" she asks.

"Oh, plenty," I say, hopping off the stool and scuttling away to hide in my room.

Yet even here, there's no chance of stewing in my own private shame, because Ryan saunters in, causing the flimsy wardrobe to wobble as he leans against it. "So what's this about you going back to the boats for the day?" he asks, raising a brow.

"I'm just spending some time with Bella," I reply. "She's been a bit bored since we left."

He nods, studying the stack of cardboard boxes I haven't got around to unpacking, because I still can't think of this place as home. Whereas Ryan is obviously delighted to have a proper bedroom instead of a tiny cabin, and has already stashed away his stuff *and* plastered the walls with posters, bought with his earnings from the gardening place. "Maybe I'll come with you," he says, turning to look me in the eye.

My heart thumps. Does he suspect something's not quite right?

"Why would you want to do that?" I frown at him.

He shrugs, still leaning on my wardrobe, so tall now he nearly reaches the top of it. "Well, I'd like to see Tyler and Jake. . ."

"Yeah, OK," I say briskly, turning away to fold clothes from my basket of clean laundry.

When I glance back at Ryan, he's still peering at me. "What?" I say crossly.

"It's just . . . why don't you stay longer at Bella's? If you're going all that way, why not hang out with her for a few days?"

I shrug. "Oh, I just fancy going for the day, really. . ."

He smirks and narrows his eyes. "And why's that?"

"What's the problem?" I shoot back. "I just told you, I—"

"I know," he cuts in, "but what's the *real* reason why you only want to be away for a day?"

I jut out my chin. "There isn't a 'real reason'. I've told you, I just *do*."

"Yeah," he sniggers, raking back his sun-lightened hair, "and I know what it is. . ."

I feel sick now. Did Ryan overhear me talking to

Bella late last night? "It's because you can't bear to be parted from your *boyfriend*," he guffaws.

"What?"

"You don't want to be away from Leon, do you?" He grins, obviously delighted with himself for embarrassing me.

I shrug, overcome with relief. "Maybe," I mutter.

"Aw, you're in love," he chuckles before ruffling my hair in a *deeply* patronizing way, then marching out of my room.

"That's some crush she's got," I hear him announcing to Mum in the living room.

"Leave her alone, Ryan," she says. I don't care, though. He can tease me about Leon as much as he likes. It suits me just fine that he thinks I've turned into a pathetic girly who won't spend more than a few hours with her best friend, because she can't bear to be parted from a boy.

He's right about one thing, though. When I'm with Leon, living here doesn't seem quite so bad. In fact, sometimes, I can almost imagine unpacking some of these cardboard boxes, and starting to make it feel like home. I don't just want to be Leon's friend, either. I want so much more, and can only hope he does, too. . .

And if Ryan assumes that's why I don't want to stay longer with Bella? Well, I'll just let him believe that. It saves me from spouting any more lies – and I think I've told enough of those for one day.

*

That night, Leon and I plot our journey. He checks train and bus times on his laptop at home, while I write it all down in my bedroom. It's a hot, airless night, and I've kicked off my duvet in favour of a thin cotton sheet. "So we're all ready for our day trip," Leon says when he calls. I can't help laughing at that. *A day trip* — it sounds harmless, doesn't it? A whole lot less daunting than sneaking off to a boatyard with no idea of what we'll do when we arrive.

"Josie," Leon says, "what d'you think will happen when we get there? If Lily-May really is Promise, I mean?"

"I . . . I don't know," I reply. I haven't even figured out how we'll get on board to check out the boat, but I don't tell Leon that.

"Maybe that's when your mum should get involved," he suggests.

"Yes, of course. I'm sure it'll all work out OK." This is what I tell myself every time my courage starts to wobble.

We fall silent for a moment. "So d'you want to come out?" Leon asks.

"What, tomorrow?"

"No, I mean now."

"But it's nearly midnight," I remind him.

"That's the best time," Leon laughs. "If I come over now on my bike, d'you think you could sneak out?"

I lie still for a moment, listening for movement in

the other bedrooms. "Well, I think Mum and Ryan are asleep, and I heard Vince asking the last customers to leave about half an hour ago. . ."

"Come on then," he says. "It'll be fun."

"But where will we go?"

"You'll see," he says, finishing the call. As I fling on a thin sweater over my PJ top and swap my PJ bottoms for jeans and canvas lace-ups, I wonder what's possessing me to do this – to creep out in the middle of the night. But then . . . aren't we doing something *far* more daring the day after tomorrow? Compared to that, this is nothing. Tiptoeing out of my room, I check that all the bedroom lights are off, then quietly let myself out of the flat. I tread lightly down the wooden stairs and pad across the darkened pub. By the time I step out into the warm, muggy night, Leon is already there, waiting for me with his bike.

"Hop on then," he says with a grin, patting the saddle.

"You mean . . . we're both going on that?"

"Yeah. It's fine."

"But. . ."

"Listen," he says, "how many times d'you think I've been nagged to give my sisters rides on this thing? I'm used to it."

I smile, even though I was really going to say, *But what about helmets?* It was drummed into me, Bella and the others that we must never cycle to school without them, and we all accepted that. Funnily enough, our parents were far more relaxed where water was concerned, and never batted an eyelid about us swimming in the river or lake. "I'd better be quick," I add, "in case Mum wakes up. . ."

"It's fine, we won't be long," Leon says. He's right, too – it *does* feel fine, once we've sped away from Castle Street with him standing to pedal and me on the saddle, gazing at the city at night. We're not even on the road. He zips along pavements, shooting down a narrow alley that brings us to a river I never knew existed. "This is beautiful," I say as we cycle along the gravelled path at the water's edge, the river shimmering with reflections from the street lamps. "I didn't even know it was here."

"Most people don't," Leon says, turning to cycle over an elaborate iron foot bridge. "When they think of rivers in London, they assume there's only the Thames. But there are loads of secret places like this."

As we cycle on, I spot a familiar building peeping through the trees. "Is that your summer house?" I ask.

"Yeah."

"Wow. I didn't realize the river's at the bottom of your garden."

"It's so overgrown down there, we tend to forget," he says. I'm amazed by all of this. Not just that there's a hidden river minutes from the Bald-faced Stag, but that the whole city looks so beautiful at night, even if there aren't any stars. "We should get back," I say finally.

"What, already?"

"Yeah," I sigh as we turn away from the river. "So, are you sure you want to come to the boatyard with me?"

"Of course I am," he replies.

"I have enough money for our train and bus fares," I add.

"I've got some, too. Mum pays me a bit for helping out with the business."

I smile, determined to enjoy every last minute of this bike ride as we zip along the quiet back streets. "I can't believe we're actually going to do it," I add.

"Not having second thoughts, are you?"

"No, of course not. I *have* to do this." I really do, I decide as Leon stops at the pub's front door and we say our whispered goodnights. Sneaking off to the boatyard really does feel like a kind of dare, and my stomach fizzes with excitement every time I think about it. But I know it's serious too. After all, we're trying to find out what really happened to Promise.

So how can that be wrong?

CHAPTER
Twenty-one

Despite my late night, I'm up extra-early and find Mum in the pub kitchen, chopping up vegetables in preparation for the lunch-time rush. Without asking if she'd like any help, I grab a peeler and start to scrape the pile of carrots for her casserole. It feels easier than just hanging around, trying to act normal, while worrying that my lies are written all over my face.

"Vince and Maria reckon I'm their star chef," she tells me.

"You're their *only* chef, Mum," I say with a smile.

"OK – there is that." She chuckles. "You're a great help, you know."

I shrug. "It's all right. I like doing kitchen stuff with you."

"Unless it involves dead mice," she sniggers, reminding me of Operation Clean-Up.

"Yeah, well, maybe not that." It's true, though: now we've degreased the kitchen, it's actually quite a nice place to be. There's usually a big pot of some kind of stew bubbling away, which Vince said is going down really well with the regulars. When we arrived, everything was frazzled in the deep-fat-fryer. No wonder the place smelled so bad.

Mum is setting out the ingredients for pastry now – her home-made fruit pies are already gaining their own fan club amongst the pub regulars – and I can sense her glancing at me. "Looking forward to seeing Bella tomorrow?"

"Oh, yes," I say, tipping the carrot peelings into the bin so she can't see my face.

"You've seemed much happier lately," she adds.

"Have I?" My voice sounds unnaturally high, but perhaps I'm just imagining that.

"Yes, definitely." She pauses. "Looks like you're getting on well with Leon, too. . ."

"Uh-huh," I murmur, wiping down the worktop, even though Mum has obviously done it already.

"I'm glad you're making friends, love."

"Well," I say with a rueful smile, "*one* friend."

She pushes back a twist of fair hair with flour-dusted hands. "It's a start, though, isn't it? And I'm sure you'll soon get to know some of the girls around here, too. Maybe I could ask Maria what kind of places Chantelle goes to during the holidays."

I nod and grab the brush to sweep up a few stray peelings from the floor. "You really like him, don't you?" Mum adds.

"Who?"

"Leon, of course," she says, laughing.

"Um, yeah," I say, as casually as I can, when "like" doesn't start to cover it. I mean . . . I like sweet pastry and strawberries, and Bella's mum's home-made lemonade. I liked leaping into the still, cool lake in the forest. But with Leon, it's more than that. . .

"Ooh, something smells delicious in here." Maria has appeared, all dangly gold earrings and a thick perfume cloud.

"Chicken casserole," Mum says with a smile.

Maria nods approvingly. "I'll be having some of that. So, how are things with you, Josie?" she asks kindly. "It's far too nice a morning for you to be cooped up in this stuffy kitchen . . . why don't you hang out with Chantelle?"

"It's OK, thanks," I reply quickly. "I've got stuff to do here."

Mum turns and squints at me. "Come on, Josie — what d'you have to do exactly?"

"Er. . ." My mind goes completely blank.

"She's going shopping with Gemma later," Maria adds. "I think you've met her, haven't you?"

"Um, yes . . . in the park." I decide not to add that she and Chantelle spent the whole time quizzing me about the inner workings of boat toilets.

"Well, there you are, then," Maria says, patting her crispy-looking hair. "I'm sure they won't mind you joining them."

I glance from Mum to Maria, panic juddering in my chest as I try to dredge up a reason not to hang out with those two. In fact, I'd rather spend the afternoon scrubbing stains off the pub carpet. "I don't have any money," I mutter.

"Yes, you do," Mum says. "You've got all that birthday money stashed away. Go on, Josie – didn't we just say it'd be nice for you to get to know some of the girls around here before school starts?"

Um . . . yes, but this isn't quite what I had in mind. . . "Mum, I don't *need* anything from the shops," I mutter, turning back to my floor brushing.

"Oh, here they come now," Maria says cheerfully at the sound of girls' voices in the pub. She pokes her head around the kitchen door. "Chantelle, come here a minute, darling. . ."

"What is it, Mum?" Chantelle appears in the kitchen in her tiny shorts and top, her blonde hair piled up with plastic clips and her eyes smudged with lashings of smoky shadow. Her expression hardens as she sees me.

"Take Josie shopping with you, would you?" Maria says. "She's at a loose end, sweeping the kitchen floor, poor thing. . ." She chuckles kindly.

"Honestly," I protest, "I've got plenty to do here."

"Like what?" Mum asks, frowning.

"Like, er . . . I was thinking of sorting out my room."

"Oh, come on, love," she insists, "you'll have fun."

Chantelle fixes me with a cool stare. "You can come if you want," she says flatly.

Oh hell. How can I wriggle out of this? "You'll enjoy showing Josie round the shops, won't you?" Maria goes on. "She doesn't know the area very well yet."

Chantelle nods glumly. "You ready then?" she says, raising an eyebrow.

"Um. . ." I glance around the kitchen, racking my brains for an excuse as to why I can't possibly go. Like . . . I am *dying*.

"Go and get your bag, Josie," Mum says. "Looks like Chantelle's ready to go."

I open my mouth and close it again. Great − so I'm going to spend the rest of the day doing something I don't remotely want to do. And, worse, I'll be doing it with someone who looks as if she'd quite happily stamp on my foot.

The whole time, Gemma has been lurking in the pub, waiting for us. Although she seems slightly less hostile than Chantelle, "awkward" doesn't begin to cover it as the three of us set off for the shopping mall. For one thing, Chantelle and Gemma look like they're going to a party or something, while I'm in ancient frayed denim shorts and a plain grey T-shirt (well, I was peeling carrots twenty minutes ago). So anyone passing would check us out and think, who's the one in the middle, with no make-up on and her hair in a mess? They'd know, just by looking, that I don't belong.

"So," Chantelle says airily, "what's happening with you and Leon?"

My heart jolts. "Nothing," I reply. "We've just been hanging out, that's all."

Chantelle makes a snorty noise and casts a quick glance at Gemma. "Just hanging out? Like, you're not going out with him or anything?"

I blink at her as we turn into the main road with all the bustle of buses and lorries unloading. "We're just friends," I say.

"Oh, right," she says with a sneery laugh. "Is that all?"

What *is* she on about? I want to say I've changed my mind about shopping and hurry back home. But that would feel like giving up before we've even got there, and how would I explain my sudden reappearance to Maria and Mum? Anyway, we're almost at the mall now. It looks pretty dismal from outside, and as we head in through the glass doors, it's obvious that this is unlikely to be a thrilling shopping experience. Half the shops have shut down, and the ones that are open are hardly enticing. I need to keep my money for tomorrow, anyway. Apart from our train and bus fares to the boatyard, I'll feel better about the whole thing if I have a bit of extra cash. The thought of possibly seeing Promise again is the only thing that's keeping me alive today.

We venture into a clothes shop where everything

seems to be encrusted with sequins. It's dazzling, like drowning in tinsel. As Chantelle marches off to flick through the rails, Gemma hovers beside me. "So what's the thing with you and Leon?" she murmurs.

"I've already explained," I say, trying not to sound unfriendly. "There isn't a 'thing'."

She peers at me through a heavy fringe. "Chantelle used to go out with him, y'know."

I frown at her. "Really?"

She nods. "She dumped him – broke his heart."

"Oh," I say faintly, wondering what on earth I'm supposed to do with this information.

"I think it's horrible, really," she adds, inspecting her black patent pumps.

Now I'm *really* confused. "What – that she finished with him?"

"No," she declares, fixing me with greenish eyes. "I mean, what he's doing to you."

"But he's not doing *anything*, Gemma. What d'you mean?" Across the other side of the shop, Chantelle holds a shiny red dress up against herself and pouts into the mirrored wall.

"The way he's hanging out with you to make Chantelle jealous," Gemma continues. "I mean, you're new here and don't know anyone and he's all over you. I just think that's *so* rotten of him."

I blink at her, stuck for words. Do I believe this? What about last night, when the two of us cycled alongside the hidden river? Chantelle doesn't know we did that. So how could he possibly have been trying to make her jealous?

Gemma has turned away to check out some sky-scraping shoes, leaving me feeling slightly sick in sparkly hell.

"I'm going to try these on," Chantelle announces, trooping back to us with an armful of tops and tiny sequinned skirts. "What about you, Gemma? Found anything?"

"No," she replies, "there's nothing I like."

"Oh, come on, Gems, there must be *something*. Get some stuff and try it on with me." I see it then – the flicker of fear shooting across Gemma's face. She is actually scared of her friend. Obviously, Gemma does whatever Chantelle wants. "Er, OK," she says, grabbing at a horrible T-shirt with a glittery Eiffel Tower on the front that happens to be hanging nearby. They totter off into the changing room together, and I can hear squeals and giggles in there as Gemma exclaims, "Oh, you look amazing, Chantelle!"

"Do I?" Chantelle simpers.

"Yeah, you're just like a model." *Ew.* Feeling queasy and overheated now, I perch on the plastic chair outside the changing room.

"You look like a bored boyfriend, love," cackles one of the assistants. I raise a faint smile and get up to browse the rails, pretending to be deeply interested in a shimmery dress with a huge red bow on the front, like a present.

What am I doing here anyway? At least tomorrow, I'll be far away from all of this. Now, though, I can't ignore the tiny seed of doubt that Leon might not be all he seems. It's so important that I can trust him – but now, after Gemma's little announcement, I'm not sure I do.

CHAPTER
Twenty-two

Finally, Chantelle and Gemma emerge from the changing room. While Gemma admits she can't afford anything, Chantelle clomps towards the till with a pile of tops. "Let's get something to eat," she announces as we leave the shop. "How much money d'you have, Josie?"

"Not much," I fib. In fact, Mum practically forced me to bring all of my birthday cash – but I'm determined to save it for tomorrow. "Anyway," I add, "I'm not really hungry. Think I'll head back home now, OK?"

"Oh, come with us!" Chantelle exclaims. "We'll just go for a pizza or something."

"Er, I haven't got much money," Gemma starts.

"Neither have I," I add, but Chantelle is already looping her arms through ours – yes, even mine – and marching us out of the mall and round the corner, into a small, cosy-looking Italian restaurant called Gino's. "Don't worry," she says, a little too loudly. "I've got plenty of cash." She flashes a fake smile as an elderly waiter approaches us. "Table for three, please," she says, and there's an embarrassing scraping back of chairs as we're shown to a table at the window. It feels all the more awkward because we're the only customers in the place.

Although it's a different restaurant, it reminds me of the one I came to with Mum, the day we bought the metal detector. Mum had let me choose whatever I wanted from the menu, and when she saw me hesitating over whether to have a dessert, she said, "Go on, Josie. How often do we have a girly day, just the two of us?"

Which is, I guess, what this is – a girly day. But one that feels all wrong. . . "I'll have this one, please," Chantelle tells the waiter, obviously unable to pronounce the name of the pizza she wants, but having sussed that it's the one with the most toppings. "You'll have the same, Gemma?" It comes out as an order, not a question.

"Yes, fine," Gemma says.

"Have you decided?" the waiter asks pleasantly, turning to me.

I feel my cheeks surging hot as I blink at the menu. Ordering any main course would gobble up a big chunk of my money, and I desperately need it to get to the boatyard tomorrow. "I . . . don't feel very well," I say quickly. "Could I just have an orange juice, please?"

The grey-haired man smiles kindly. "Of course you can, dear."

Chantelle gives me a quick frown. Then, as the waiter

leaves our table, she calls after him, "Could we also have two side orders of garlic bread, dough sticks, coleslaw and, er . . . some olives?"

The waiter gives us a bemused smile. "Shopping's hungry work, eh, girls?"

"Oh yes," Chantelle says with a cheesy grin. What's she trying to do – chomp her way through the entire menu? And what the hell has happened to *me*? I never used to find myself in crazy situations like this. But now I'm sitting in the kind of restaurant your mum might bring you to for a treat, with two people I have nothing in common with. And, worse, one of them went out with the boy I've hardly been able to stop thinking about lately, *and* I bet she doesn't even like olives. . .

"So," Chantelle says loudly, "that loo you had on the boat—"

Oh no, not that again. . .

I give brief, flat answers as Chantelle fires more toilety questions at me: "Did it stink? What happened when friends came round, weren't they grossed out?" Amazingly, the topic doesn't put her off shovelling great slabs of pizza into her mouth when their meals arrive. The table is crammed with delicious-looking food, and I'm actually hungry now – but of course, after saying I'm broke and feeling ill, I can hardly ask for a bit of their pizzas or side orders. Instead, I start wondering how much of Chantelle's thick foundation will come off when she wipes that tomato sauce smear from her chin.

"Just going to the loo," I say, jumping up from my seat. I don't really need to go. I'm just desperate to get away from these two and all that scrummy-looking pizza and garlic bread, which I'm not even allowed to touch. As I make my way across the restaurant, I try to ignore my hollow, rumbling tummy. When I glance back, Chantelle and Gemma are leaning together, whispering. About Leon, probably. Or chemical loos. Well, let them, I think defiantly as I head into the ladies' and lock myself in a cubicle.

Will all the girls at my new school be like this? While Ryan seems fine about the new term starting soon – he's already met a couple of girls in his year who work at the gardening place – I can't imagine how I'll ever fit in. Chantelle will spread word around that I lived on a boat, like it's some shameful secret, and before I know it, it'll be "Are you a gypsy then?" and all that stuff. It makes rescuing our boat – if Lily-May really *is* ours – feel even more crucial. I sit on the loo with the lid down, trying to figure out how to make my excuses and leave as soon as possible.

By the time I'm back at our table, all the plates have been cleared away. Chantelle and Gemma are now tucking into towering ice-cream sundaes smothered in whipped cream and chocolate sauce. My stomach growls jealously.

"Mmmm, this is *lovely*," Chantelle says, in a fake, swoony voice.

Gemma nods, looking decidedly pale and clammy. "Another Coke, please," Chantelle calls across the restaurant to the waiter. "Want one, Gemma?"

"Er . . . yes, please," she says timidly. Meanwhile, I'm so hungry I could munch our bowlful of sugar cubes, like a ravenous pony. I glance at the door, wishing I could launch myself through it and charge home as fast as possible. I want to be helping Mum in the kitchen, or even listening to Ryan bragging on about how brilliant everyone thinks he is at work. *Anything* but being stuck here with these two. . .

And then . . . everything seems to change. Instead of the three of us being in a restaurant, around the corner from a shabby shopping mall, it feels as if we're in a terrible scene from a film. The waiter comes over and places our bill on the table on a white saucer, then wanders off to arrange a vase of flowers on the window sill. "I feel sick," Gemma whispers, clasping a hand over her mouth. She *does* look ill – despite her thick make-up, her whole face has gone a weird greeny colour. Then, just as the waiter heads into the kitchen, shutting the door behind him, Gemma opens her mouth, and out comes . . . a great, gushing pile of vomit. There's so much of it, it seems as if it's never going to stop. And no wonder: this is what a twelve-inch pizza, two Cokes, side orders of coleslaw and garlic bread and a sundae consisting of three flavours of ice cream, warm chocolate sauce and a sprinkling of broken crunchy biscuits look like when they're all mushed up and half-digested.

"Oh my God!" Chantelle screams.

"Are you OK?" I exclaim, gawping at Gemma's distraught face, then at the pile of sick on the floor.

"No!" Gemma wails. "I feel awful. . ."

"Let's get you outside," Chantelle says quickly, "in case you do it again."

As she leads Gemma out of the restaurant, I crouch down on the floor and try to clear up the mess. It's hopeless, though, attempting to mop up the stinky puddle with paper napkins from our table. All I manage to do is add piles of wet tissue to the soupy mess. "I'm really sorry," I mutter, leaping up to my feet as the waiter reappears. He glares at the floor. "What happened here?" he barks.

I just shrug. He is obviously furious, and who can blame him? It might not be my fault, but he doesn't care about that. "For goodness' sake," he growls, shaking his head. "Where have your friends gone, anyway?"

"Outside for some fresh air," I whimper as a man with three chattering kids pushes open the restaurant door and ushers them in. When he spots the pool of sick on the floor, he quickly herds them back out again.

The waiter stomps off and returns with a mop, a bucket, some cloths and a spray. *Hurry up*, I will Chantelle and Gemma. *Come back in so we can pay the bill and get out of here.* But there's no sign of them. The waiter gives the saucer with our bill on a little nudge, obviously keen for us to pay up and leave. "Er . . . I'll just go and see where they are," I say.

"No, you stay here and *I'll* look," he announces, marching across the restaurant and out on to the busy pavement.

I can see him through the glass door, peering up and down the street. Then my focus switches to Gemma's chair, where her leopard-print shoulder bag was hanging. It's gone. I glance at Chantelle's seat and realize her bag has gone too, and so has her carrier bag from that clothes shop. *The two of them have taken all their stuff.* Why would they do that? As the truth dawns on me, I almost stop breathing. This feels horribly different to when me and Mum were out having ice-cream sundaes together, chattering happily with the metal detector parked beside us.

The waiter has come back inside and is marching up to my table, red-faced and furious. He snatches the bill from its saucer and waggles it at me. "Can you pay this, please?" he snaps. "Looks like your friends have gone home without you."

"But . . . they can't have." I stare at the figure on the bill. It amounts to all the money I have, not just in my purse, but the *world*. The waiter is glaring at me, breathing noisily through his hairy nostrils. "I only had a drink," I say, realizing how pathetic that sounds. What does he care about who had what? He just wants his money.

Blinking back furious tears, I open my purse, count out the money and place it on the saucer. There it goes: the money from Auntie Sheila in Manchester, my shadowy New Zealand grandparents, Bella's mum and dad, Maggie and Phil from the boat opposite ours, and Tyler and Jake's parents . . . all of it. In fact, when the waiter counts it up, I'm a little bit short. I scrabble about in my purse but there's nothing left.

"That'll do," the waiter says gruffly, picking up the saucer piled with money. Something else – a flicker of sympathy, perhaps – crosses his face. "Some friends, huh?" he says.

I nod, barely capable of speaking. "Yeah."

He narrows his eyes and gives my arm a pat. "Weren't in on their little prank, were you?"

"No," I whisper. "I had no idea."

He nods, his face softening. "I can tell. Off you go then, love. I hope your day gets better."

"So do I," I mutter. As I leave the restaurant and step out into the sunny afternoon, I realize I'm no longer hungry after all.

CHAPTER

Twenty-three

I keep my head down all the way home. Not because I'm worried about being spotted by Chantelle or Gemma (after all, they're the ones who should be mortified, not me) but because I want to hide from the whole world. What an idiot! OK, the puking obviously wasn't intended, and I'd felt sorry for Gemma at that point. But stuffing their faces, ordering the most expensive pizzas and heaps of extras – *that* was planned. Obviously, Chantelle had intended to do a runner all along.

I try to call Bella but her phone is switched off. It wouldn't seem right, calling Leon about this, especially after what Gemma said about Chantelle breaking his heart. Do I believe that? I'm not so sure. But right now, it feels as if there's *no one* I can talk to.

By the time I'm back at the Stag, I've worked myself up into a furious rage. I'm all set to track down Chantelle, or at least Vince and Maria, to explain what's happened and demand my money back. But apart from two elderly customers chatting over their beers, the only person in the pub is Alex, the shy Polish barman who helps out sometimes. I bark a quick hello before hurtling upstairs to find Mum.

She's in the kitchen, and the smell which fills it is so lovely and sweet, it brings a lump to my throat. It's that pastry smell from our last boat party, when Mum had packed me off to school and spent all day baking. "Are you OK, Josie?" She peers at me across the dingy room.

"Er . . . it's just. . ." I clamp my mouth shut.

"Sweetheart, what *is* it?"

Without warning, my eyes fill with tears.

"Have those girls been mean to you?" she asks. "Oh, love, I could tell you didn't really want to go. I just thought it would be good for you to spend some time with them instead of hanging about here. . ."

"I'm fine," I say quickly, turning away so she can't see the tears spilling down my cheeks.

"Josie, you're *not* fine." She marches over to me and places her hands on my shoulders. "Please tell me what's happened." I pause for a moment before it all spills out: the pizzas, the puking, and the girls leaving me with the bill. "That's disgusting," Mum exclaims, hugging me. "I can't believe anyone would be so mean. Right, I'm going to call Vince right now. . ." She turns away and reaches for the phone.

"No!" I cry.

Mum frowns. "Why not? We can't let them get away with this."

"But you've only just started working here, and we don't know how Vince will react if you complain about his daughter."

"We've got to do something, Josie," she says, shaking her head.

I link my arm through hers. "Yes, I know, but not right now, OK? I'll get the money back somehow. Let's not just . . . dive in and cause a big scene. Anyway, maybe I should have realized what they were up to. . ."

"It *wasn't* your fault," Mum says sharply. Still looking annoyed, but obviously considering that the Stag is the only home we have, she sighs and lifts down a large plastic box from on top of the fridge. Before she has even taken off the lid, I can guess what's inside. "Look good?" she asks.

"Perfect," I breathe, gazing at the strawberry tarts.

"Just keep the box flat on your knee while you're in Charlie's truck, OK?"

Now, of course, I'm *choking* with guilt. Since when did life become so horribly complicated? "Nothing ever happens around here," Bella declared once as we lay on Tarragon's deck, and I agreed that, for a couple of thirteen-year-olds, our lives were tragically uneventful. Right now, I'd give anything to have that ordinariness back again.

Mum smiles, putting her arms around me and holding

me so close, I can feel the beat of her heart. "Maybe I shouldn't have pushed you into going shopping with those two," she murmurs.

I force a smile that feels as fake as the vase of faded yellow plastic tulips on the window sill. "I just don't think I'm their kind of person, Mum," I say.

She kisses the top of my head. "Never mind, darling. I'll figure out a way of discussing it with Vince or Maria and, anyway, you'll have the whole day with Bella tomorrow. *That'll* put the smile back on your face."

CHAPTER
Twenty-four

Just before I go to bed, I call Leon to tell him I can't afford our trip. "We can still go," he says. "I told you I've got some money."

"But you can't pay for our fares and everything!" I exclaim. "That doesn't seem right."

"I *want* to come with you," he insists. "It's my choice, isn't it? And it won't cost that much."

I hesitate. It still feels slightly wrong, but how else am I going to get there? While Ryan is earning plenty of money, he'd never give me so much as a bean without a full interrogation of what I needed it for.

"What happened to your money, anyway?" Leon asks.

I pause. "Er . . . I had to use it for something else."

"Right. Well, it's not a problem unless . . . you haven't had a change of heart, have you?"

"No, of course not!"

"'Cause if we leave it much longer, the boat'll

probably be sold, won't it? I've just checked the website again and it's still on there at the moment."

I can't help smiling at that. "You really care about this, don't you?"

"You know I do," he declares. "So, will you call me when you're at the bench in the morning, like we said?" Where we first met when I handed back Daisy, he means.

"Yep," I reply.

"OK," he says. "Good luck."

"It'll be *fine*," I say, trying to sound far bolder and braver than I feel.

In fact, next morning, everything goes like a dream. Mum is preoccupied making steak pies and curries in the kitchen. I keep popping in, hoping to time my announcement for when she's busy with everything bubbling away, needing constant attention. That way, she won't be able to take much notice of me.

"Mum," I say, poking my head around the kitchen door for about the fourth time, "Charlie's just texted me – he's here. . ."

"What, outside?" She's grappling with a huge cooking pot filled with simmering tomatoey liquid.

"Yeah, I've got to go now, though. He's in a real hurry—"

"Oh, hon, tell him I'm sorry, I'd love to see him, but maybe next time they're in town. . ."

"OK, Mum." I force a big, bold smile, give her quick

kiss on the cheek and leg it through the pub to the main door.

"Josie, wait!"

I whirl round to see her standing there in her sauce-splattered white apron. "What is it, Mum?"

She has put down the pot and is holding out a transparent plastic box. "You forgot the tarts, silly girl."

"Oh, right." I almost cry with relief as I take them from her.

"Have fun," she adds before darting back into the steamy kitchen.

Once outside, I charge down the street, terrified that Mum will decide to pop out and say hi to Charlie after all. It's all starting to feel horribly real now – less of a dare or an innocent day trip, and more like a completely mad thing to do. I run all the way to the scrubby little park by the florist's, the tarts bashing around in their box, and land heavily on the bench. "Leon?" I say, gripping my phone. "I'm here now."

"Right – give me five minutes."

I slip my phone into my pocket, noticing the odd passer-by glancing at me, and feeling horribly self-conscious all on my own with my bag at my feet and a plastic box on my lap. As I wait, I mull over what Gemma said about Leon using me to make Chantelle jealous. Was she just making the whole thing up? If so, why would she *do* that?

Leon is striding towards me now, and as his face

breaks into a huge grin, I quickly push the dark thoughts away.

"Hey." He lands beside me on the bench. "So you did it, then. You managed to get away."

"Yeah." I nod. "It wasn't too difficult."

His gaze drops to the box on my lap. "See you've brought supplies," he says with a laugh.

"Yeah, Mum insisted I bring them because she knows they're Bella's favourite." I sigh as my gaze meets his. "That made me feel terrible, even more than all the lies. But I've kept reminding myself why I'm doing this — that it's for all of us."

Leon nods. "And your mum still doesn't know about the boat on the website or anything?"

"No, not a thing. If she knew I was doing this, she'd have a heart attack." I dig my toe into the ground.

"It'll be all right," he says gently. "She'll understand when you explain everything."

"Yes, I know." Mustering a smile, I stand up, still clutching Mum's box of tarts. "Think you'll be able to help me get through this lot on the train?"

Leon laughs, and tiny sparks shoot through me as his bare arm brushes against mine. "I'll see what I can do," he says.

CHAPTER
Twenty-five

Of course, no one thinks there's anything out of the ordinary about a boy and a girl on a train in the summer holidays. We're just two friends on a day out, eating home-made strawberry tarts, drinking Cokes and looking out of the window as the scruffy buildings eventually make way for green, open countryside with the occasional village snuggled in-between fields.

I glance at Leon, trying to imagine him with Chantelle, but I just can't make them fit together in my head. *He's hanging out with you to make Chantelle jealous,* Gemma said. Would anyone actually do that? Chantelle doesn't even know we're doing this today, so he can't be here for any reason other than he wants to be.

I sense him looking at me. "Nervous about this?" he asks.

"Not really. Not yet, anyway." We're sitting opposite each other at a table for four. As there's an old lady next to me and a younger woman beside him, I feel kind of awkward talking about it.

"It'll be OK," he says. "We'll just have a look. You're not planning to confront him, are you?"

I shake my head, wishing we could talk about something else. So I ask him about his little sister, Rosie, and whether the dare game is a regular thing of theirs. "Oh, yeah," he laughs. "She's mad about it. The thing is, though, she's completely fearless, so I have to be careful about the dares I give her – because she'd go right ahead and do them."

I snigger, realizing it wasn't entirely true when I said I wasn't nervous, and wishing I were a little more like this five-year-old kid. "If Bill sees us," I add under my breath, "I'm sure he'll recognize me from that day we first brought Promise to his yard."

Leon nods. "Well, maybe I should be the one to go in and ask to see her."

"Yes, good idea." I relax a little, impressed, as I always am, when Leon refers to a boat as "she". "Er ... and then what?" I ask.

He laughs and finishes his Coke. "I have no idea. Look – we're slowing down. I think we're coming into Braidford."

"What, already?" The journey has flown by and the tarts have been scoffed. We get up and make our way towards the door.

"Excuse me!" the old lady calls after us. "You've forgotten this." She's waving the plastic box of crumbs.

"Thanks," I say, hurriedly taking it from her. As soon as we've jumped off the train, I drop it into a litter bin. "Sorry, Mum," I murmur.

"So . . . where to now?" Leon asks as we make our way through the station. It's the nearest one to Bill's boatyard. For the rest of the journey to Clingford, we have to take a bus.

"This way," I tell him. "It's not too far – just a two-minute walk." In fact, I know Braidford well. As well as coming to the big multiplex cinema here, it's where we'd change from the bus to the train on our rare jaunts to London. There's an arched metal bridge which leads us past a row of smart-looking shops, to where the country buses stop.

I almost ask for tickets to Issingworth as we climb on to the bus – the small town where my old school is, and the closest place to our old mooring on the river. But we're going further today. As Leon buys our tickets and the bus pulls away, it starts to sink in what I've really done.

I've told so many lies, and what exactly do I plan to do when we get there? What chance do we have of making everything right? It's a breezy, sunny day, the dazzling blue sky streaked with thin white clouds. London, and the Stag, feel a long way away. "You'll see the river where I used to live," I tell Leon. "We might even spot Bella and Murphy."

"Really?" He looks delighted by this, but to me, this

whole situation is starting to feel weirder by the minute. In fact, as the bus trundles along the winding country lanes, I start to feel distinctly queasy too – possibly from stuffing my face with six strawberry tarts on the train, but more likely due to Gemma's announcement about Leon and Chantelle yesterday. OK, so it's none of my business who he's been out with in the past ... but surely he could have mentioned it? I am living above her parents' pub, after all.

I stare pointedly out of the bus window.

"You OK?" Leon asks.

"Yeah, I'm fine."

"Can't be long now, can it?"

I shake my head, and we fall into an awkward silence. It wasn't like this when we cycled alongside the river at night, or hung out together in the summer house. Now, though, perhaps because I'll soon be face-to-face with Bill McIntyre, I can't shake off a horrible sense of unease.

"There *is* something wrong," Leon says, fixing his gaze on my face.

I blink at him. "Well, something happened yesterday," I mutter.

Leon frowns. "What?"

I blow out air as we pass through an impossibly pretty village, all rose-covered cottages like something out of a picture book. "I went shopping with Chantelle and Gemma and they decided they wanted a pizza, so. . ." As it all pours out – the puking incident, and me having to pay for everything – Leon sits there, aghast.

"God, that's awful," he says when I pause for breath. "I can't believe they did that! Why didn't you say?"

"I. . ." Peering down at my fingernails, I wonder how best to put it. "It wasn't really anything to do with you."

"But. . ." He looks genuinely hurt now. "We're friends, aren't we?"

I shrug.

"*Aren't* we?" he repeats.

"Yes, but. . ."

"There's something else, isn't there?"

Leon stares at me as I shift uncomfortably in the seat. The bus rattles along, taking a sharp corner too quickly and hurtling down a steep hill. My stomach swirls uneasily. "Gemma told me that you were Chantelle's boyfriend," I say quietly.

"Did she?" Leon says.

"Yeah. Is it true?" I ask, quickly adding, "I know it's none of my business but, you see, after the thing in the restaurant, and way Chantelle behaves around me, it might just. . ." I break off and shrug. "It might explain a few things."

Leon exhales. "I'm sorry, I should have told you. . ."

I slide my eyes towards him, wondering what's coming next. "My parents used to be good friends with Vince and Maria," he starts, "which might surprise you. . ."

I nod.

"Well, Mum hasn't always been as posh as she makes out she is. But, as soon as the business started raking in the money a couple of years ago, she decided to reinvent herself. She got herself a whole new look, and started mixing with people who could promote the business." As he smiles ruefully, I wonder what this is all leading to. "And she decided Vince and Maria didn't really cut it as friends any more," he goes on. "Dad just went along with it. It's Mum who rules the roost in our family, as you might have gathered."

"Uh-huh," I murmur. "I haven't even met your dad."

"Well," Leon continues, "that's why Chantelle acts so weird with you. You see, we used to have all these holidays together with them. We went to Greece, France and Sicily together, all over the place, really. Chantelle could never be bothered with any of my sisters. . ."

"Why not?"

He laughs. "You've met them, haven't you? They're pretty feisty – Rosie especially – and don't like being told what to do. And, as you've probably realized, Chantelle only likes people who do what *she* wants to do."

"Like Gemma," I remark.

"Yeah, exactly."

We fall silent again, and I realize I've been so engrossed in what Leon's been telling me that I hadn't even noticed we're nearly at the river now, and that soon we'll glimpse the boats. "So," I say, hardly daring to ask, "what happened between you and Chantelle?"

He pauses, those coffee-coloured eyes sending a rush of butterflies fluttering in my stomach. "We were just mates, messing around on the beach together," he says. "But last summer, things changed. It was pretty obvious that Mum didn't want to be in Corfu with Vince, Maria and Chantelle. She thought they were beneath her."

I nod, encouraging him to go on.

"As the days went by," he continues, "there was a definite feeling that this holiday would be our last one together. At least, it was obvious to Chantelle and me. So, one evening, we went down to the beach on our own to try and figure out what was going on. And it felt kind of sad, you know? Like an ending."

I nod. Oh yes, I know all about those.

"And . . . we kissed that night," he murmurs, looking down as his cheeks flush. "We were sort of together the rest of the holiday, and she was different then – not hard and full of herself like she usually is."

I take a deep breath, reflecting that that's not *quite* the story Gemma told me. "What happened when you came home?" I ask.

He shrugs. "Er. . . this is going to sound *really* bad, but I realized I'd made a huge mistake. I didn't want her to be my girlfriend. Me and Chantelle . . . sure, we were mates, but we're totally different people. It was never going to work."

Ah, now I get it. Although I've only known her for a

few short weeks, I can imagine exactly how Chantelle reacted to this. "So she wasn't too happy," I suggest.

Leon shakes his head. "This makes me sound awful."

"No, it doesn't," I murmur.

"Well . . . she did take it badly," he says quietly.

"Was she really upset?"

"More like furious, bombarding me with texts and calls. Kept going on about what people would say when they knew I'd dumped her — which I hadn't, really. The holiday thing had only happened because the whole family situation felt so weird. Anyway," he continues, "her parents weren't impressed either, because they think their little princess should have whatever she wants. So that really finished things between our families. Although Chantelle likes to make a big thing of us still being friends. . ."

As Leon stops and looks at me, I feel as if a little bird is fluttering around my heart. "I wish you'd told me all this before," I say.

He nods, looking shamefaced. "I didn't want you to think I'm the kind of person who gets close to someone, then just dumps them."

I turn this over in my mind. So he cares what I think of him, which might mean he wants to be more than friends . . . or am I reading too much into this? "So what was with the big public display of affection in the Stag?" I ask.

He frowns. "What d'you mean?"

"Um…" I pause, hoping I don't sound horribly jealous. "Well … I saw her throwing her arms around you in the pub, that first time you came round for me…"

"Oh, God." He laughs and shakes his head. "She kind of sprung it on me. I did think it was weird – but now I suspect it was for your benefit."

"What, to warn me off?" I ask with a grin.

Leon shrugs. "Just one of her little games, I guess."

"But why—" I stop abruptly, all thoughts of Chantelle evaporating from my mind as I glimpse a flash of bright colours down on the river. "Look, that's where I lived!"

"Oh, wow. It looks amazing. Which one's Bella's boat?"

"The green one."

"You were so lucky," he declares. "I'd *love* to live on a boat." I turn and smile at him. That day when we'd left the river, I'd truly believed my luck had run out. I'd never imagined I'd meet a boy who would make me feel as if anything was possible. He's right, too. It does look amazing down there – even more amazing than I remembered. The river is as flat as a sheet of glass, and there's not a soul around. There's a space next to Tarragon, too, where Promise was moored. The new boat must have moved on.

"That's Kate, Bella's mum," I announce as she emerges through their cabin door. She is glancing around with a hand shielding her eyes in the sun, and looks as if she's calling to someone, or something. And she *is*. Moments later, a little peanut-butter-brown terrier shoots out from the trees and scampers along the path towards her. "There's Murphy!" I yell. "Look, Leon – that's my dog!" I leap up without thinking, overcome by an urge to tell the driver to stop so we can jump off and run down to the boats. But instead, the driver shouts, "Could you just SIT DOWN? No messing about on my bus."

"Sorry," I say, falling back on to my seat and grinning at Leon. "It's just so good to see him, you know? It feels like *ages*. Oh, I miss him so much."

"Yeah, I can imagine. Anyway," he adds, "if all goes to plan today, maybe you'll be seeing him a lot more."

I nod, hardly daring to hope that Promise might possibly be ours again, and that the Stag, and Chantelle, and a horrible-looking school I haven't even started at yet, could fade away as if they'd never been part of my life.

There's someone I'll never forget, though. As the bus climbs the hill away from the river, I turn to look at Leon. Sure, it seemed as if my whole life was over a few weeks ago. But now, it feels as if something else is just beginning.

CHAPTER
Twenty-six

It's early afternoon by the time we arrive in Clingford. The walk from the town centre to the boatyard isn't as far as I remembered and, by the time the big blue and white sign saying "McIntyre Boat Repair & Maintenance" comes into view, my mouth feels so dry I can hardly swallow. "I'm not sure about this," I say quietly.

Leon gives me a concerned look. "D'you still want me to go in and have a look around first?"

I pause for a moment, twisting Bella's thin silver ring around my little finger. "No, let's go in together."

"Are you sure? What if Bill sees you?"

"What if he does?" I say, sounding braver than I feel. "I'm sure we'll think of something."

"OK," Leon says. Now *he's* the one who looks a little unsure.

"So let's go," I say, marching along the overgrown lane towards the huge wooden shed. The yard is strewn with bits of rusty machinery, and we step carefully around them as we make our way to the shed door. It's all splintered and rotting at the bottom, and creaks loudly as I push it open. After the brightness outside, it takes a few moments for my eyes to grow accustomed to the gloom.

"Can you see anything that looks like Promise?" Leon whispers as we both peer around the cavernous shed.

I shake my head, checking each boat in turn as we wander past. Some are half-painted and a few are gleaming proudly, perfectly restored. But most of the boats look ancient, as if they've been dumped here when there's no hope for them at all.

"It's sad," Leon says, as if reading my mind. "Most of these look like wrecks."

"Yeah." I nod. "Promise definitely isn't here, though – these are all a lot more modern. There's nothing like her at all." I keep glancing down towards Bill's glass-partitioned office at the far end of the shed, even though there's no sign of him so far. We pace around, checking the whole place one more time. "What if we're too late," I say, my insides feeling as heavy as lead now, "and he's sold her already?"

"But the website—" Leon starts.

"Well, perhaps he hadn't got around to updating it."

He nods. "Then . . . I don't know. Maybe we could still track her down somehow. . ."

That's what I love about Leon: the way he manages

to convince me that there's still hope. Like he cares as much as I do. "He probably has some kind of book," I say, "where he keeps details of the people who've bought boats from him. . ."

". . . Or it might be on his computer," Leon says eagerly. "Shall we try and find it?"

"I saw it. It's in his office."

"Can I help you?" barks Bill as he looms into the shed.

My heart leaps, and I try to compose my face into something like a normal expression. "Er . . . we were just passing by and thought we'd have a wander around," I say brightly. How dumb does *that* sound?

His thick dark eyebrows swoop down. "Yeah, well – it's not a playground. You can just wander right out again."

"No, I know that," I say. "It's just. . ." I tail off. *Think, think. . .* "My dad saw an advert for a boat on your website," I explain in what I hope is a confident voice. "He's on his way to have a look. We're supposed to be meeting him here." Bill squints at me, probably wondering why I've changed my story. I swallow hard and glance at Leon.

"Which boat are you talking about?" Bill asks.

"Er. . ." The name! It's whizzed right out of my head again.

"Lily-May," Leon says quickly.

Bill's face sets in a scowl. "Lily-May," he repeats slowly,

and I see a flicker of recognition in his small, dark eyes. *He remembers me from when I came here with Mum,* I think. "She's been sold," he growls.

"Oh," I say flatly. "Oh . . . I see."

"Your, um . . . your dad'll be so disappointed," Leon remarks to fill the tense silence. He turns to Bill. "He's really keen, you see. He's pretty sure she's the boat for him."

"Yeah, well, he can be as keen as he likes," Bill replies, "because she was taken away a couple of days ago."

"D'you know where to?" I ask.

Bill shrugs. "No idea. None of my business, is it?"

I nod and start to make for the door. "OK. Well . . . thanks anyway."

"Thought your dad was meeting you here?" Bill calls after us in a sneering tone. He knows we were lying all right.

"I'll call him and tell him there's no point," I reply as we step back outside, where the day already looks a little less perfect.

CHAPTER
Twenty-seven

We trudge in silence along the tree-lined lane that leads back to the main road. The blue sky has turned grey now, as if washed over with murky ink. "Are you OK?" Leon asks gently.

I nod. "Yeah. I just feel . . . kind of stupid." I stop and look at him.

"You shouldn't," he says. "We tried, didn't we? We did our best."

"Yes, but. . ." I tail off as a cool breeze whips through my long dark hair. "I should have phoned the boatyard this morning to check if Lily-May was still there. I just didn't think of it. Guess I was more concerned about getting here. . ."

"It's not your fault," Leon insists.

I exhale loudly. "But it's been a complete waste of time, hasn't it? And you've spent all that money on our fares, too."

Tears prickle my eyes, and I look down so Leon can't

see. "That doesn't matter," he says firmly.

He's right, I suppose. There are far bigger things to worry about, like all the lies I told at home. "Mum's bound to find out," I add glumly. "Next time she speaks to Charlie or Kate, she'll mention my supposed day with them on the river, and they won't know what she's talking about." I glance back up at Leon. "She'll be horrified when she finds out. She'll never trust me again."

"Yes, but you did it for all the right reasons," Leon points out. "When she realizes that, she'll understand."

I turn this over in my mind. "Are some lies OK, d'you think?"

"Of course they are," he says firmly.

Fine rain begins to fall as we start walking again, hitting our faces like damp breath. "Bill knew we were lying," I add. "I'm sure he remembered me."

Leon nods. "He couldn't wait to get rid of us."

I glance at him, glad he's here with me, despite everything. "D'you think that means Lily-May really *was* our boat, after all?"

"Possibly."

"Or am I just being stupid and hoping too much?"

"No, you're not," Leon says. "I only wish there was something else we could do."

We've reached the town centre now, and although Leon buys us each a bag of chips, I can hardly manage to eat them. We pass the museum where Mum and I saw the beehive, and head for the park with the pointy-roofed cafe. As we sit at a small table with a Coke each, the day I came here with Mum floods back into my mind. After the bad news about Promise, it felt as if she just gave up. And I'm not prepared to do that yet. "Leon," I say carefully, "we've come all this way, so I think we should keep trying. Keep looking for Lily-May, I mean."

His face brightens. "You mean, try to track down the person who bought her?"

I take a sip of my Coke. "Maybe. I mean, it could be someone local, couldn't it? Lots of people have boats around here, and boaters usually notice when a new one is moored nearby. Probably because not much happens when you live on the river."

Leon smiles, and I sense my spirits rising. Somehow, I've managed to uncarth a little sliver of hope. "I don't want to be like Mum and just give up," I add firmly. "Anyway, I'm going to be in so much trouble when all this comes out. It can't all be for nothing."

Leon finishes his drink and gets up from his seat. "Let's go, then. There's still plenty of time before we need to start heading back, so how about we follow the river as far as we can?"

"Yes, good idea," I say as we step back out into the park. The drizzle has stopped, and a chink of sunlight is forcing its way between puffy clouds. "You know what?" I add. "I still have a good feeling about today." I look at him, and the smile that lights up his deep brown eyes makes me feel that *anything* is possible.

"Well," he says, making sparks shoot through me as he grabs my hand, "let's start looking right now."

CHAPTER
Twenty-eight

As we make our way down to the river, I wonder if I've really gone crazy this time. For one thing, we are holding hands. It doesn't seem real. I keep at glancing at Leon, and he keeps looking at me, and it's a wonder I haven't actually burst with happiness. We're not talking now. The two of us are too intent on scanning the riverbank, as if Lily-May will materialize magically before our eyes.

There are plenty of boats – scruffy little cruisers, the odd cheerfully painted narrowboat – tied up along the riverbank. But there's no beautiful antique one made from nut-coloured wood. In fact, I'm starting to think that my imagination has run away with me, and that Promise really was sent off to be broken up at the scrapyard, just like Bill McIntyre said.

The sun has come out properly now, forcing its way between overhanging branches and dappling the tree-lined path. As it leads us out of town, back towards

Bill's boatyard, it becomes so narrow we have to drop hands and walk in single file. I'm in front, scanning the greeny-tinged river ahead. "Look," I say as a bright-red narrowboat appears around a bend. "Maybe they've seen something." We stand and wait until the boat is almost alongside us. "Excuse me," I shout, "have you seen a wooden boat called Lily-May?"

It's an elderly couple on board. The man frowns, adjusts his peaked cap and says something to the woman beside him. "Don't think so, love," he calls back.

"Are there any boats up that way, towards the boatyard?" I ask.

They are chugging away from us now, and I hurry along the path to keep up. "Not that we noticed," the woman says, looking bemused. Then she turns to the man and says something to him, before calling back to me, "Actually there was just one, round the corner."

"What was she like?" I'm now having to jog to keep up. Leon has stopped on the path and is throwing open his arms as if to say, *What are you doing*?

The man laughs. "My dream boat," he says.

My heart leaps. "OK – thanks!" I look back at Leon, who's striding towards me.

"What did they say?" he asks.

"They passed something on the way – the man said she was his dream boat. . ." I grin. "I think we should have a look, don't you?"

"Yeah, of course."

184

I try not to get my hopes up as we hurry along the riverbank. After all, "dream boat" could mean anything. While we always regarded Promise as perfect, occasionally I'd heard a passer-by murmur, "Look at that old thing – can you imagine living on that?" Leon and I fall into silence as we follow the bend of the river. My phone bleeps with a text, and I stop to read it: *How u getting on?* Bella asks. *Any news? Desp to hear!*

Nothing yet, I reply while Leon continues to scan the river ahead.

"Hey, Josie," he says suddenly. "Look at that." We both peer into the distance, where a boat has come into view. It's wooden, yes, but around twice the size of Promise, with gleaming brass-edged windows, and it's covered with so many pots of brightly coloured flowers, you can hardly see the deck at all. It's a floating palace – the kind our boater friends would drool over when something similar chugged past our mooring. "Oh," I say flatly. "*That's* a dream boat."

He puts an arm around my shoulders and fixes me with one of those smiles that light up his whole face. For a split second, I think he's going to kiss me. It certainly feels as if something amazing is about to happen. My heart skips, and my breath catches in my throat. "Well, I think it looks like a heap of trash," he quips.

"No it doesn't," I shoot back.

Leon shrugs. "I guess some people might go for that kind of thing," he says, grabbing my hand again and starting to hurry along the bank, "but I still think it's a bit flashy."

I frown at him as we march along, unable to tell if he's joking or not. Further ahead, Bill McIntyre's garish blue and white sign peeps out between thick branches.

It's then that I see what Leon is getting at. Tucked behind the huge, posh boat is a much smaller one, which was hardly visible from where we were standing. But now we're closer, I can see the familiar curve of a hull, the row of narrow windows and the slightly upturned, pointed bow.

"So what d'you think?" Leon asks.

I'm running now, having pulled ahead of him, hardly daring to hope. My phone bleeps again, but I ignore it this time because I'm pelting along as fast as I can, past the big wooden boat, stopping abruptly as I reach the smaller one tied up beside it.

"It's Lily-May!" I cry.

"I know, I can't believe it!" He stops abruptly at my side.

My gaze skims the polished wooden hull. Her name has been carefully painted in swirly black letters on her side. As for the hull, instead of being a warm, nutty shade all over, there are paler sections which are obviously brand new. This boat looks like she's been patched up – incredibly well, I have to admit, and recently, too. You can almost smell the fresh varnish.

"Could this be Promise, d'you think?" Leon asks.

I push bedraggled hair from my eyes. "I still don't know. The shape is right, but see the door that leads down into the cabin? It used to be green, not that burgundy colour, and it was all scratched and rotting a bit, too. . ."

"Maybe it's been replaced," he suggests.

I nod, then check both directions to make sure no one's coming along the path. The only living thing in sight is a lone duck, swimming lazily in the middle of the river. "C'mon," he urges me, "what are you waiting for?" Leon leaps aboard, wobbling slightly, as people tend to until they're used to the rocking motion. I burst out laughing as I join him on the deck.

"I can't believe this," I say, gazing around in wonder. "The deck is exactly the same, apart from some new bits here, and here. . ." I point at the paler planks of wood.

He focuses on my face. "So . . . *is* this your boat?"

I open my mouth, momentarily stuck for words. "This sounds stupid, but . . . I still don't know for sure. I mean, there were loads of dents and scratches on Promise. There was a pretty serious crack running along the deck here." I indicate the smooth, freshly varnished wood. "And see the windows? Their frames were silvery metal before, and now they're black."

"Shall we go in, then?" Leon asks impatiently.

I nod and reach for the door's handle. "It's locked," I announce, trying it again in case it's swollen in the hot weather and has just got a bit stuck. "We hardly ever locked up," I mutter under my breath. "We just kept the key on a nail by the door."

Of course, there's no key here today.

I step back as Leon gives the door a rattle. "Could we prise it open, d'you think?" he asks.

"I wouldn't like to try. It would probably damage it. Hang on, though, there *is* another way in. . ." I run to the bow, followed closely by Leon, and crouch down at the large, square hatch. "Help me with this," I say, trying to hook my fingers into the tiny gap to prise it open.

"Won't that be locked too?" Leon asks.

"I don't think so. If this really *is* our boat, then there isn't a key. Murphy knocked it into the river ages ago and we didn't bother getting a new one."

"I think it's jammed, then," Leon mutters as the hatch still refuses to budge.

"It probably is. We never really used it." I sigh, looking around for something to force it open.

"Er . . . would this help?"

I drop my gaze to the small red object he's produced from his jeans pocket. "A knife!" I exclaim. "What are you doing with that?"

He laughs. "Oh, they're handy, y'know. I was showing Rosie how to use it the other day."

I don't know what amazes me more – the fact that a five-year-old is allowed to mess around with a Swiss Army knife, or that I'm lucky enough to have found a friend like this. "You let your little sister use that?" I ask incredulously.

Leon shrugs. "Yeah, to whittle wood. It's part of her education."

Before I can completely embarrass myself by babbling about how brilliant he is, Leon has flicked open one of the blades and is using it to try and force open the hatch. "Nope," he mutters. "Still won't budge. Hang on a minute. . ."

"Leon, stop," I hiss. "Someone's coming." A man with a dog has appeared from around the bend. As Leon quickly assumes a casual, cross-legged position on the deck, I perch on the cabin roof as if simply enjoying the afternoon sunshine.

"Hi," the man grunts as he passes us, his dog zigzagging in front of him on its lead. "Nice boat."

"Thanks," I say with a forced smile.

He walks on, and as soon as he's out of sight, Leon flips out a little pointy implement from his knife. "What's that for?" I ask.

"Rosie asked me that," he chuckles. "She's obsessed with this knife. I told her it's for getting stones out of horses' hooves, and she said, 'Why d'you have it then? 'Cause we don't have a horse. . .'" I watch intently as, in one deft movement, he pushes it into the tiny space and prises open the wooden hatch. I help him to lift it away, then jump down into the cabin below, with Leon landing beside me a moment later. Reaching up

189

through the square opening, he carefully slides the hatch back into its closed position.

We stand in silence, blinking in the dim light as we peer around the cabin. It feels the same – it even *smells* right. "I think this was Mum's cabin," I whisper, pushing open the door and stepping into the main living area. "This *is* Promise," I exclaim, too thrilled to keep my voice down now. "Leon, it's definitely our boat!" I gaze around, and everything is just as it always was: our little kitchen with the oven and sink and the worktops with their speckled blue pattern. There are the long, built-in seats on each side, made of dark, shiny wood, and the red cushions, which are a perfect fit. Maggie made them for us when Mum decided Promise needed a spruce-up last winter. "Are you sure?" Leon asks, pushing back dark, wavy hair from his eyes.

"Of course I am. Come on – I'll show you the other cabins." We peer into Ryan's, then finally mine. "My mirror's still here!" I shriek.

"That's amazing. Why wouldn't he have taken it down?"

"Because it wouldn't come off the wall," I say, feeling like laughing and crying all at once. "When she bought it, Mum used some kind of strong glue instead of bothering to drill holes, and she had to leave it behind when she cleared out all our stuff." I glance at my flushed, wide-eyed reflection in the mirror, its sparkly butterfly border matching the ones that are fluttering

madly in my stomach right now. "My God," I breathe.
"I can hardly believe this. I'm so glad you're here to
see it too." It's true — I'm *loving* being able to show him
my real home. It's almost like seeing Promise through
Leon's eyes and, perhaps for the first time, I can see how
magical she really is.

"What about your tin, then?" Leon asks.

"OK." I swallow hard, realizing now why I've left this
part till last. I'm scared, you see — scared in case it's gone.

"Did you say it was under your bed?" he prompts me.

I nod as, slowly, I bob down to reach under my old
wooden bed and lift the loose slat. But before I can feel
around for the tin, there's a loud clunk above us, and
the boat rocks violently. Someone has just stepped on
board.

CHAPTER

Twenty-nine

I wish I were somewhere else. I wish I were . . . I don't know. Stuck at home in my mustard room, or in that bleak shopping mall with Chantelle and Gemma . . . *anywhere* would be better than this.

Leon squeezes my hand tight. There's another thud as someone else steps on to the deck. "She's looking good, Bill," comes a booming male voice I've never heard before. "You've done an excellent restoration job on her."

"Well, they do say I'm the best in the business." Bill chuckles, and I can sense the tiny hairs on the back of my neck sticking up. There's the sound of a key in the door as it's opened up, then footsteps as the men come down the short flight of wooden steps into the cabin.

"So what was her history again?" the other man asks.

"Oh, she came in for repair a while ago," Bill replies. "Owned by some clueless hippy-dippy woman who thought she might need a small repair to the hull." He snorts with laughter. "And of course, once I'd got this beauty out of the water, I could see we were talking major work. She wouldn't have been able to afford it."

I glance at Leon, feeling as if my blood has turned to ice.

"So she sold her to you?"

"Yeah, as a wreck," Bill says. "But I was happy to do a full restoration. As you know, David, she's a very special boat."

"*Sold* her?" I mouth at Leon. Of course, there was no money involved – just a pack of lies. My heart is thumping so hard, I'm amazed the men can't hear it. They're so close now, I can hear every creak from the wooden floorboards as they move around. I can even hear Bill breathing noisily through his nose. Any second now, they'll peer into this tiny cabin. . .

I bite my lip, wondering if we'd be able to hurtle straight past them and escape. No, that would be impossible. There's hardly any space out there, and they could easily block our way out. "Well, Bill," the other man is saying, "you've been true to your word – she's turned out better than I could have hoped. I'd like to go ahead and buy her."

"Great," Bill says. "If you could transfer the funds into my account later today, you can take her tomorrow. She's completely finished and ready to go."

The other man clears his throat. "And . . . you're not prepared to budge on the price?"

"Oh, come on," Bill says with a gravelly laugh. "She's already a steal – you know that."

The boat rocks again as first one man heads back upstairs to the deck, followed, miraculously, by the other. There's the metallic sound of the door being locked, and a soft thud as each man jumps on to the path. Their voices fade as they make their way back along the riverbank towards the boatyard.

I let go of Leon's hand. "They've gone," I announce, my heart still rattling away at what feels like three times its normal speed.

He shakes his head, laughing softly in disbelief. "We are *so* lucky. . ."

We stand there, blinking in the shadowy cabin for a few moments, before I lift the loose slat and reach into the space behind it. As my fingertips touch a hard metal lid, I stop. No one found it. It's still there. My hands are shaking as I carefully lift it out.

"Leon," I say, my vision fuzzing with tears, "I'd like you to meet my dad."

I know it's risky, and that Bill could come back at any time. Even so, it wouldn't feel right, hurriedly showing Leon the contents of my tin. So we perch on the edge of the hard wooden bed while I hand him each object in turn: the newspaper cutting about Dad being an athletics champion, and the picture of him as a little boy in what was probably his parents' back garden, where he's busy making a complicated-looking model boat. There are more photos, taken during camping holidays and Christmas parties. In one, he's just the way I remember him – smiling proudly, his dark hair neatly cropped, standing on Promise's deck with a baby in his arms.

The baby is gazing up adoringly at him, her eyes wide and her mouth open in one of those funny gummy smiles babies do. "That's me," I tell Leon.

He smiles. "You haven't changed a bit."

"Apart from now I have teeth," I laugh, handing him the Seven Wonders of the Ancient World book, which he leafs through slowly, taking care to study each one of Dad's soft pencilled drawings.

He turns to look at me. "So what shall we do now?"

"I . . . I don't know." Yet, as soon as the words leave my mouth, I realize I *do* know. "We're going to take her, Leon."

"What . . . you mean take Promise?"

I nod. "Yes."

He tips his head, studying my face. "But . . . how? Where would we go?"

"Home," I say simply.

CHAPTER
Thirty

"You mean to London?" he asks. "Wouldn't that take all night?"

"No," I say, "I mean back to where we used to live. There was still a space there, next to Bella's boat, remember? She mentioned that someone else had moored there, but they must have moved on."

"How long will that take us?"

"A couple of hours, I think." I look at him, hardly daring to believe I've suggested this, but knowing it feels right. After all, I'm only planning to take back what belongs to my family. Then it will all come out that Bill lied to us, cheating us out of our home so he could make a fortune. "Will you come with me?" I ask hesitantly.

"Of course I'll come!" Leon exclaims. "Are you crazy? Where else d'you think I'd go?"

"I don't know. I just—"

"How will you start the engine, though?" he cuts in. "Does it have a key or something?"

"Yes," I say, "and Bill must have that. But there is another way to start it — with the crank handle. It's not easy but if Mum could manage it, I'm sure I can too. We kept it in a compartment under the deck. Let's see if it's still there. . ."

Putting the lid firmly back on my tin, I place it back under the bed. Leon follows me out of the cabin and, being taller than I am, he reaches up to push open the hatch. Once he's shoved it aside, we haul ourselves up through the opening and on to the deck, where I lead him to the smaller hatch, with its storage compartment underneath. Just as I thought, the crank handle is still here. Back below deck, I fit it to the engine. I can't get it started at first but finally, as I push with all my strength, there's a low spluttering noise, as if Promise is clearing her throat after waking up from a long sleep — and the engine kicks into life. "It's going!" Leon yells from outside. "You've done it!"

"Course I have," I laugh, scrambling back outside and joining him on the deck again. I inhale deeply, taking in the familiar warm, oily smell of the engine. It really feels like coming home. "Could you untie her?" I ask Leon.

"Sure." He jumps on to the bank, lifts the rope from the mushroom-shaped bollard and steps back on to the deck. My heart feels as if it could burst with joy as I take the tiller and guide her gently away from the bank.

"You know this'll take ages, don't you?" I tell Leon.

"I mean, even after we've moored next to Bella's boat, we'll still have the journey back to London tonight. . ."

"So?" he grins.

"I just thought, in case anyone starts to worry, maybe you should call home."

He shrugs. "I don't think they will."

I smile and give his hand a squeeze. While I'm glad Leon has so much freedom, it still doesn't feel right that no one cares. I'm also starting to worry that Bill could come back at any time and find his prized boat gone. It's the first time I've wished that Promise could chug along a *little* faster. . .

Still gripping the tiller with one hand, I slip my phone out of my pocket and read the text that came earlier: *Any news???* "Bella again," I explain. I'm about to reply, but where to start with all that's happened today? No, better to just turn up and surprise her.

"So," Leon says, "d'you think it'll be OK, leaving Promise at your old mooring?"

"Yes, there are plenty of people there who'll keep an eye on her. Anyway, I need to get back and tell Mum."

"Don't you want to phone her now?" he asks.

I shake my head. "Can you imagine how she'd react? No – better to tell her face to face. Then I can explain everything properly and she won't freak out." I glance at Leon, aware that he's studying me with a quizzical look on his face. Is it because I've taken his dare further than he'd ever imagined, or does he think I've gone completely nuts? I'm about to ask if he's OK with all of this when he does something that takes the words right out of my mouth.

Without any warning at all, he leans forward and gently kisses my lips. My head swirls, and Promise does a crazy curve in the river as I forget how to steer for a moment. In fact, I forget everything apart from the boy I'm with now.

Although we're puttering along as slowly as the duck beside us, I feel as if I could soar like a bird.

CHAPTER
Thirty-one

The sun beats down as we leave Clingford behind. Soon we're out in the countryside, surrounded by nothing but gently sloping hills and a wide turquoise sky. As for that kiss — well, I feel as if I'm sort of glowing all over. Oh, I know things are about to get complicated. Bill will probably track us down — it's generally not too difficult to find a boat, after all. But what we've done today still feels absolutely right.

As I guide Promise past a tiny overgrown island guarded by a swan, I keep stealing glances at Leon. Those deep brown eyes, those long, dark lashes and infectious smile ... how can I start to doubt what we've done when he's here? "So we've done it," he says with a grin.

"Yeah." I blow out air. "I can't wait to tell Mum now. She'll understand why I had to sneak off today."

"And what about Ryan? How d'you think he'll react?"

I mull this over for a moment. "I don't know. He likes living at the Stag – he has his job, more money than he's ever had in his life, and he's started to make friends." I smile and wave as we pass a narrowboat heading upstream. "But this is our home, Leon. Promise is ours and we need to have her back."

"Yeah," he says, "of course."

"I don't know what Bill McIntyre will do when he discovers she's missing," I continue. "It's a lot of money to lose. But he can hardly report it to the police, can he?"

"Not when she wasn't even his to sell," he agrees. I catch his eye, wondering what'll happen when we're back home – not just with Mum and Promise, but to Leon and me. I do want our home back, but I also wish today could go on for ever: our own perfect little world, with no Chantelle, and no difficult questions to answer. . .

"Can I steer for a while?" Leon asks.

"Sure," I say, moving aside so he can take the tiller. "Just keep an eye on the bow to see if we're veering over to one side. . ."

"You think I'm going to crash her, don't you?" he teases.

"No," I laugh, "course I don't. But you do realize you're in sole charge of a very valuable boat right now, don't you?"

"Stop pressuring me," he laughs as we pass a

family gathered around a picnic table on the riverbank.

"Look," I add, "they're all watching to see if you mess up. You should have L-plates."

We carry on like this, chattering and bantering, while I feel as if I could burst with happiness. Occasionally, I forget about Bill McIntyre and the whole stack of lies I told, and almost believe we really are on a day trip. Just a boy and a girl, boating on a perfect summer's day . . . until, suddenly exhausted after the day's events, I stretch out on the warm deck. Soon I'm drifting away, lulled by the low rumble from the engine and the relentless heat of the sun. . .

"Josie!" Leon's cry wakes me with a start.

"What's wrong?" I scramble up to my feet.

"Nothing," he laughs. "Sorry, I didn't mean to shock you. It's just . . . well – is this starting to look familiar to you?"

I glance towards the boarded-up building to our right. "That's the old boatyard we used to go to! Yes, it's not far now. About fifteen minutes."

Rubbing my eyes, I take back the tiller from him, my heart thudding hard now as we pass familiar landmarks: the old-fashioned garage which I'd cycle to for newspapers and milk, and the posh hotel with its immaculate garden where prim-looking adults are having afternoon tea. "That's where Mum worked," I tell him.

"Bit different from the Stag, huh?" Leon says with a smile.

I nod, aware of a small twist of sadness deep in the pit of my stomach. Of *course* I want my old life back. I miss Bella like crazy, and Murphy too. We were all happy on the river – I even got the impression that Ryan enjoyed moaning about the lack of space. But now, it's hitting home that, in rescuing Promise, I could lose the loveliest boy I've ever met. . .

That kiss replays in my mind, and I sense myself blushing. As if tuning into my thoughts, Leon takes my hand in his. "You know," he says softly, "I've never met anyone like you."

I laugh, aware of my cheeks turning an even fiercer shade of pink.

"No, really," he insists. "I mean . . . I dared you to call the boatyard, didn't I? But you didn't just do that. You planned the day, you sneaked off and confronted that man. . ."

"I was terrified in the boatyard," I remind him.

"OK, but then you actually *stole* the boat. . ."

"Rescued," I correct him, then gasp, "Look, we're here!" All bunched up together, the boats look like an explosion of paint colours against the sludgy greens of the surrounding water and trees.

"Which side shall we moor on?" Leon asks.

"The right bank. There should be room next to Bella's. . ." I squint into the distance, reassuring myself that of course there'll be a space there for us. No boat was moored there when we passed on the bus, on our way to Clingford – I definitely checked. But now, as we slow down and draw closer, I can see that another boat – a dark blue cruiser with a shiny white roof – is crammed into the space next to Tarragon. "There's a boat in our old mooring," I announce. "We can't stop there. . ." Anxiously, I scan both sides of the river.

"Aren't there are any spaces at all?" Leon asks.

"Can't see any."

"There must be *somewhere* we can stop. . ."

I shake my head, panicking now. "There are hardly any official moorings on this part of the river, and you can't just pull up anywhere – not where there's nothing to tie up to. . ." This is precisely why, once someone's finally managed to get a mooring here, they hardly ever leave.

I slow Promise right down. A few of the boaters are pottering about on their decks, but no one has spotted us yet. Then Tyler, who's lying flat out in a pair of shorts on his deck, turns to see who's approaching. Maggie swivels round too, and soon several boaters have emerged from their cabins to see who's arrived. I'm focusing so hard on Bella's boat, I don't even smile or shout hello. "We'll have to double moor," I tell Leon. "There's nowhere else to go."

"What does that mean?" he asks.

"Instead of mooring at the bank, we'll tie up against another boat. I'll get as close as possible to the green one, OK? That's Bella's. Take the rope, then jump on to her and tie it around the railing as quickly as you can."

"Sure," he says. He grabs the rope and is poised, ready to jump. "Just tell me when. . ."

"Josie?" comes Tyler's voice from across the water. "What are you doing here?"

Right now, I'm concentrating so hard on guiding Promise in gently alongside Tarragon, I can't even reply. "Jump!" I yell at Leon.

We're beside Bella's boat now, and Leon leaps on to her, quickly tying us up to the railing which runs the length of her gleaming deck. I switch off the engine and breathe out a huge gasp of air. "We've done it!" I exclaim.

Leon's back beside me now, looking impressed. "That was tricky," he says with a grin.

I'm about to say it was nothing really, because I've been handling Promise for as long as I can remember, when Tyler shouts again from his boat. "Josie? What's going on?"

I throw open my arms as if to say, *Where do I start?*

"That's the boat we saw in the yard!" Maggie calls across the water. "It's not Promise, is it, Josie?"

"Yes, it is," I yell back.

"We thought it was! But her name—"

"Long story," I reply with an unsteady smile. I turn to look at Leon, knowing we'll soon be besieged by boaters, all demanding to hear the whole story. Then, in the distance, I see a girl with her blonde hair in tiny plaits striding along the riverbank. And she's not alone. "It's Bella!" I cry. "Leon, look – that's Bella, and she's got Murphy with her!"

My best friend stops suddenly at the sound of my voice, then her mouth falls open and a huge grin crashes like a wave across her face. "Josie!" she yells. "What are you doing here? What have you done?"

"You won't believe it," I say, vaguely aware of other boaters making their way towards us, obviously desperate to know why I've turned up out of the blue, on a boat called Lily-May, with a boy they've never seen before. Murphy has seen me too, and pulls away from Bella so suddenly, his lead flies out of her hand. She lets out a cry and charges after him, but he's running as fast as his little terrier legs can take him, along the path towards Tarragon. Leon turns to me and laughs. "He's cute. No wonder you've missed him."

"I really have," I say as Murphy pelts along the riverbank, tongue out, eyes flashing in the sun.

He leaps on board, tail wagging madly as he sprints across Bella's deck. "Murphy!" I yell. "Come here, boy—" And now he's jumped across the small gap between Tarragon and Promise – but instead of hurtling straight into my arms, he slips on the deck, his feet scrabbling frantically as he tries to regain his balance. I try to grab him but he kind of spins, slipping off the edge with his lead still on and landing in the river with a yelp and a splash. "Murphy!" I yell, stretching down as far as I can to reach him.

"Oh my God," Bella cries, jumping on to her boat and hurrying towards us. At first I'm not too worried – Murphy's a good swimmer – but then I realize that something's wrong. Although his face is just about out of the water, he's struggling like crazy and spluttering mouthfuls of river. "Murphy, swim!" I cry, turning to Leon. "I don't know what's wrong with him – he can swim really well normally . . ." I'm aware of urgent voices as other boaters approach, all shouting, telling me what to do. But they all blur into one as Murphy's head disappears under the water.

I plunge into the river and look around frantically, hoping to glimpse a flash of wet brown fur or a blue plaited lead. There's a splash as Leon jumps in too. "Murphy!" I scream.

"Can't you see him?" asks Bella, her face distraught as she peers down at us.

"No," I shout back, "we've churned up all the mud at the bottom so I can't see anything. . ."

She leaps in too, calling Murphy's name as she sweeps her hands through the water.

"Maybe he's gone *under* the boat," Leon suggests, ducking down, but coming up with nothing more than a desolate look on his face. The river is especially deep here. While Leon is tall enough to stand up, Bella and I are having to tread water to keep afloat. A strangled sob escapes from my mouth as Tyler jumps in beside me.

Four of us are flailing about in the river now, while Maggie, Phil, and Tyler's dad all shout instructions and encouragement from the riverbank. Then, above all of those voices, one rings out the clearest: "He's here!"

I turn to Leon. "You've found him? Is he—"

"Look," he says, lifting up my sodden, trembling dog, who's making the strangest spluttering noise I've ever heard.

"Murphy!" Bella and I cry in unison.

I swim through the water towards Leon. "Is he breathing? Is he OK?"

"I don't know . . . he was right under the water. His lead must have got tangled up in something." Holding Murphy high above the water, Leon wades to the bank.

"Here," Tyler's dad says, "pass him up to me." Murphy lets out a small yelp of pain as Leon hands him over. I'm trembling as I scramble out of the water, and Bella is ghostly pale.

"Oh, you poor loves," Maggie exclaims as I reach out to take Murphy from Tyler's dad.

"Maybe he's just in shock," someone murmurs.

"Is he all right?" Bella asks, shivering at my side.

"I don't know," I whisper, looking around at the

distraught faces as everyone gathers around. All I do know is that, if I hadn't decided to take Promise, none of this would have happened. . .

Hot tears stream down my face as I look down at my Murphy, a limp, wet bundle in my arms.

CHAPTER
Thirty-two

"What's going on?" It's Charlie's voice I hear first, then Kate's, as they're told by too many people, all in a rush, what's just happened. Someone calls the local vet on their mobile. Bella, Leon, Tyler and I are all lined up on the long wooden bench in Tarragon's living area, wet-haired and wrapped in an assortment of brightly coloured blankets. Maggie has clicked into looking-after-everyone mode and is busy making tea. Murphy, who's tucked into a blanket nest of his own on my lap, isn't doing much. While he's still breathing at least, I can tell something is very wrong.

"The vet will be able to help him, love," Maggie says, giving him a concerned look.

"Yes, I know," I murmur, glancing up as Charlie hurries down the steps, laden with bags of shopping, followed by Kate.

"Josie, are you all right?" Kate cries.

I nod. "Look at Murphy. I don't know what's wrong with him. . ."

Crouching down beside me, Kate gently lifts my dog from my lap and on to a cushion on the floor. Leon's hand grips mine as Murphy just lies there, making a feeble attempt to lick a front leg.

"I think he might have broken something," Charlie says.

"The vet's expecting him now," adds Kate.

"But how. . .?" I start, my eyes welling up again as I look at Leon.

"I'll take him," Charlie says firmly. "You lot need to put on some dry clothes."

"Bella has plenty of things you can wear," Kate cuts in. "Tyler, I think you should go home and get changed, and, er. . ." She glances quizzically at Leon.

"This is my friend Leon," I murmur.

Kate smiles. "I'm sure we can find you some dry things for you too."

"Oh, I'm OK," he protests with a shake of his head.

"No you're not," Kate says firmly. "I know it's summer, but you're not sitting around soaking wet – you'll catch a chill."

"Charlie," I say, "I want to come to the vet's with you. I need to be with Murphy."

He places a hand on my arm. "No, you stay here and get warmed up. Tell Kate everything that's happened. All we've had so far is a load of confused gabbling out there. . ." He nods towards the window. Out on the riverbank, a few of the boaters are still standing together in clusters, discussing the afternoon's events. And to think, we used to say that *nothing* ever happened around here. . .

Reluctantly, I hand Murphy, still wrapped in a blanket, to Charlie. He gives me a reassuring smile before carrying my dog up the steps and on to dry land. Moments later, I hear his rattly truck starting up and driving away. "I'd better go," Tyler says reluctantly, getting up from the bench. "Good luck with everything, Josie."

I muster a weak smile. "Thanks."

Squeezing on to the bench beside me, Kate puts an arm around my shoulders. "So, tell me everything that's happened. . ."

I pause, deciding there's no point in hiding anything from her. So I tell her about Leon and me and our mission, how we were nearly discovered hiding in the cabin on Promise, and how I decided there was only one thing we could do – to bring my boat home.

"Oh, Josie," she says, shaking her head.

"It was the right thing to do, though," Bella insists. "You couldn't just let Bill McIntyre get away with what he did."

"OK, Bella," Kate says, shooting her an annoyed look. I glance at Leon, then drop my gaze to the floor. All of us have pulled off our sodden shoes or sandals, and little puddles of river water have formed on the wooden floorboards.

"You don't think we should have done it, do you?" I

ask Kate as Maggie hands around more mugs of sweet tea.

"No," Kate says firmly. "No, I don't. I can understand why you did – I can only imagine how furious you were when you found out what that man had done. But, you have to understand, you just *can't* take things into your own hands like that." She fixes me with a concerned gaze.

"I know," I mutter.

She frowns and glances at Leon. "Whose idea was this, anyway?"

"Mine," I say quickly. "Honestly – Leon just wanted to come with me."

"Well," Kate says, "that man could have attacked you or anything. Can you imagine the kind of situation the two of you could've found yourselves in? And what your mum will say when she finds out?" Her expression softens as she wipes a tendril of wet hair from my face.

"I should call her," I say glumly, fishing my phone from my pocket. But of course, it's waterlogged. No sign of life at all. "I guess yours is broken too," I add, looking at Leon.

He takes it from the pocket of his drenched jeans, along with his small black leather wallet and Swiss Army knife. "Yeah, but it might dry out," he says with a shrug.

"I don't hold out much hope," Kate says briskly, jumping up from the bench. "Girls – go and get changed in Bella's cabin. Leon, you can use mine and Charlie's –

it's opposite Bella's. If you look in the wooden trunk, you'll find some T-shirts and shorts of my husband's. Can't promise they'll fit you or be your style, but now's not the time to worry about that."

With a murmured thanks, he does as she says, glancing back at me with a wry smile. "Still," he says, pushing open the door to Kate and Charlie's cabin, "at least you've got your boat back."

"Yeah." I muster a smile, knowing I'll feel a whole lot better when Charlie comes back from the vet's.

"I'll phone your mum, Josie," Kate calls through as Bella and I start to peel off our wet T-shirts and shorts in her cabin.

"OK," I reply. I glance at Bella, trying not to think about what Mum's reaction will be. And, although I try my hardest to listen as Kate makes the call up on Tarragon's deck, I still can't make out the words.

"Your mum's new boss is bringing her here as soon as he can," Kate announces as Bella and I join her outside.

"You mean Vince?" I glance at Leon, who's already decked out in Charlie's huge tie-dyed shorts and an oversized T-shirt in wild psychedelic colours. In any other situation, I'd burst out laughing.

"Yes," Kate replies, "and I should warn you, Josie – she sounded a bit upset, to say the least." With that, she disappears back down into the cabin. Soon, delicious spicy smells start to drift up from the kitchen.

As the day starts to cool and the shadows lengthen,

Bella, Leon and I stay out on deck. None of us feels like talking much. There's still no sign of Charlie, and Mum could be ages yet. "She'll understand when you explain everything," Bella says firmly.

"Well, I hope so."

"Of course she will," Leon adds. Although he throws me a reassuring look, this time, I'm not so sure he's right.

In the meantime, all we can do is wait.

CHAPTER
Thirty-three

By the time Mum arrives, looking pale and shocked with Vince and Ryan at her side, any explanations have completely flown out of my head. Her eyes are wide and sore-looking, her mouth tense and down-turned.

"So, Helen," Kate says quickly, greeting her with a hug, "this is a bit of a . . . situation, isn't it?"

"It sure is." Mum turns to me. "Josie," she starts, "I know the two of you might have thought you were doing the right thing . . ."

I inhale deeply, waiting for a massive telling-off.

". . . but there's going to be so much trouble about this," she goes on, perching on the deck beside me. "You can't just take a boat like that, even if you believe she's ours."

"I know, but—"

"You've really messed up this time," Ryan announces, shaking his head.

I glare at him in silence.

"But. . ." His mouth curls into a smile. "It's kind of amazing too. I mean, I'd never have imagined you'd dare to do something like this."

"This wasn't a dare, was it?" Mum asks sharply.

"No," I cry. "I mean, it wasn't just that. Lily-May really is Promise, can't you see?"

Her expression softens and she reaches forward to squeeze my hand. "Show me, then."

I do just that, stepping from Bella's boat on to Promise's deck. As the door is still locked, Mum, Ryan and I have to clamber down through the big square hatch. We peer into each cabin in turn, and I'm relieved that I stored my tin away under my bed. Now's not the time to surprise Mum with that.

She makes her way through to the living area, where the three of us stand speechless for a moment, as if no one quite knows what to do next. "I can't believe he did that to us," Mum says softly, sounding all choked up.

"He conned us out of our home," Ryan adds, putting a protective arm around her shoulders.

"I know," Mum says, turning to me. "I'm still angry, Josie, but I have to say, you've been very brave."

"Does this mean we're moving back to the river?" I ask hesitantly. Now it's a real possibility, I'm not sure I want to, after all.

She shakes her head, causing a tendril of fair hair to escape from its clip. "It's not that simple, love. Even assuming we can prove this boat is Promise, there's still my job and the flat, and you're both enrolled at a new school. . ."

"There's my job, too," Ryan cuts in. "We can't just give up on everything, can we? What would Vince think if you just left, Mum, after his last chef walked out?"

"Not leaving us, are you?" comes Vince's deep, throaty voice as, with some difficulty, he manages to squeeze himself down through the hatch.

"No, I'm not saying that," Mum says quickly.

He smiles kindly, scanning the room, checking out our kitchen and all its perfectly designed cupboards and seats. "Well, I hope not," he says, "although I can see that this must've been a lovely place to live. Like being on holiday all the time, huh?" He chuckles kindly.

"Erm . . . sort of," Mum laughs.

"Not so sure about the chemical loo, though," he adds with a grin. Now Bella and Leon have joined us, too. Our old living room is starting to feel a little crowded.

Vince has sidled up beside me. "I heard about Chantelle and Gemma's little prank in the restaurant," he murmurs.

"Did you?" I croak.

He nods. "Your mum told me. I'm really sorry, Josie. I've had a stern word with Chantelle, and we'll make sure you're not out of pocket."

"Don't worry about it, Vince," Mum says quickly.

"You've been kind enough to drive me all the way here today. That's enough—" She stops abruptly, and we all flinch at the sound of an urgent male voice outside.

"*Look – there she is!*"

"Who's that?" Vince asks over the sound of an approaching engine.

Leon peers through a window. "There's a boat coming with two men on it. . ."

"Quick," Mum says, "let's get out." One by one, we hoist ourselves up through the hatch, and jump from Promise to Tarragon as the boat approaches.

It's Bill, and another younger man. His son, maybe. Both look furious. "What'll we do?" I cry.

"I don't know, Josie. . ." Mum grips my hand tightly.

"I'll get him," Ryan says, clearly trying to sound bolder than he feels.

"No," Mum snaps. "You'll only make things worse."

The air is filled with the whine of their engine and a rich diesel smell. "Pull up alongside the boat behind," Bill commands from the flimsy-looking motorized dinghy. The younger man expertly guides in the boat, allowing Bill to leap across an ageing navy blue narrowboat and on to the bank, where he quickly secures their rope around a bollard.

Both men storm on to Tarragon and glare at us. "What are you doing?" Kate barks, marching right up to them with a ladle in her hand. "This is *my* boat. Get off or I'll call the police."

"Oh, I don't think you will," Bill snaps, pushing past her and stepping on to Promise. "This boat's mine. I've restored her. She was a wreck when you brought her in."

"Yes," Mum counters, looking fiercer than I've ever seen her, "and you said she was going straight to the scrapyard."

"If we'd known she could be fixed up," I add, "we'd never have left her with you."

"Leave it, Josie," Ryan says quick.

"But he was planning to sell her, Mum!" I yell. "He even had a buyer. He was coming to collect her tomorrow, I heard them discussing it."

"Get out of my way," Bill snarls, taking a key from his pocket and unlocking the door which leads down into the cabin. "You've caused us enough bother already. It should be me who's calling the police."

As the younger man goes to untie Promise from the railing on Bella's deck, Vince storms forward, his face scarlet with fury. "Leave this boat where it is," he roars. "Get off right now."

"And who are you?" Bill bellows, eyes blazing.

"Never mind who I am. Just clear off and leave these people alone."

Bill stares at Vince. Mum, Kate and Ryan are all shouting at him, but it's Vince who grabs Bill by the front of his oil-smeared T-shirt. "Are you listening to me?" Vince yells. "I know what's happened here. These are decent people and you lied to them. Now get the hell out of here."

The punch seems to come from nowhere. At first, it's impossible to tell who hit who. Someone screams, and I'm vaguely aware of Leon throwing a protective arm around my shoulders as Vince staggers back with a groan.

"Are you OK, Vince?" Mum cries. "God, you're bleeding, this looks bad. . ."

"I'm all right," Vince mutters. "Look, they're getting away. . ."

"It doesn't matter," she insists, peering at his face. "We can't catch them now."

"We should call the police," someone shouts.

"I don't know what to do," Mum cries. "I need time to think. . ."

"We should stop them," Leon announces, although none of us dares try. Instead, we all stand in bleak silence as Promise turns in a wide circle, then heads back upstream, taking my blue tin with her.

CHAPTER
Thirty-four

When Leon and I hatched our plan to rescue Promise, I'd never imagined it would end up with a black eye and an emergency operation on my dog. It's like when you tell lies – they stack up on top of each other in ways you'd never have predicted. Vince's right eye is already puffy and purple – although, when we're back at the Stag with Maria fussing over him, he almost seems proud of it. "I nearly had him," he boasts as we all cluster around a pub table, which is laden with Mum's vegetable curries and bowls of rice. Although they smell fantastic, I hardly feel like eating right now.

At least Murphy will be fine, despite fracturing his leg, presumably by hitting the side of the boat as he fell into the river. I'm not sure how we'll pay for the operation, but right now, that feels like the least of our worries. At least he's alive, and being cared for by Charlie, Kate and Bella. The surprising thing is, Vince has said he can live with us in the flat. "He needs to be with his family after a trauma like that," he says, forking in a great mouthful of curry.

"We'd like that," Mum says, smiling around the table. Apart from Vince, Maria and our own family, Leon is also here with us. When Chantelle wanders into the pub and her dad beckons her to join us, it feels like some strange, thrown-together family.

"We've talked about the restaurant incident," Vince tells her under his breath, causing Chantelle's cheeks to flush bright red.

"OK, Dad," she mutters.

"I think Josie deserves a proper apology," Maria adds firmly.

She flicks her gaze towards me. "Sorry," she says in a whisper.

"No, I mean a *proper* one," Vince snaps, and I almost feel sorry for her, surrounded by so many watchful eyes – including Leon's – not knowing where to put herself.

"Let's leave it for now, Vince," Mum says kindly, dishing up a bowlful of curry for Chantelle. No one except me notices the brief, grateful look she gives Mum.

Mum clears her throat. "I've been thinking," she says, turning to me and Leon. "What you two did was pretty crazy, but it's made me realize I gave up too easily the day we first took Promise to that boatyard." Her eyes glint as she places her fork in her bowl. "I've called the police," she adds, "to tell them there's a dispute about the ownership of a boat."

"Brilliant," I exclaim. "So what'll happen next?"

Mum grins. "I can easily prove that Promise is ours and has just had her name changed."

"But how?" I ask her.

"Every boat has a serial number on its engine, and I've got all the paperwork – I mean, the ownership papers from my granddad. And everything will match up."

"Really?" I gasp. "You mean you had the official papers all along?"

"Yes, of course," she says with a smile. *Why* hadn't I known that?

"So, what'll happen next?" Leon asks, turning to Mum.

"They're getting on to it straight away," she says calmly. "The police in Clingford know Bill McIntyre already. Although they wouldn't give me any details, they did hint that he's been involved in all kinds of disputes over the years."

"But. . ." Ryan frowns. "He won't just hand over Promise, will he? He doesn't strike me as that kind of man."

Mum smiles broadly. "He might not be, but this time he won't have any choice. The police will impound the boat, just like they do with cars, until I can get there tomorrow with all the paperwork. I've already hired a car. . ."

"I could've taken you," Vince says quickly.

"You've done enough to help us already," Mum says gratefully. "It's time we stood on our own two feet." She looks round at Ryan and me. "This doesn't mean we're going to live back on Promise like before though, OK?"

I nod, glancing at Leon. "Our mooring's been taken by someone else anyway," I tell her.

"Yes, I know," Mum says, "and anyway, I don't believe we can just turn back the clock like that. So much has happened these past few weeks, and we need time to settle down and get our lives together again." She blinks at me. "How d'you feel about that, Josie?"

I catch Leon's eye, then meet Mum's hopeful gaze. "I'm fine with that, Mum. Honestly, I really am." It's true. It feels right to be here, even though Bella is miles away on the river. I gave her the silver ring back and, even though she protested at first, I said it was important for her to have it. I feel close to her every time I look at my finger and see the faint, paler line where it used to be.

Ryan clears his throat and looks around the table. "I'm happy to stay too," he says.

"Well," Mum adds, "I think I am too. Vince, Maria – you've been really good to us. The job's a challenge, but," she chuckles dryly, "I think I can handle it."

"I knew you would," Vince says with a grin, "and I have to say, we're getting quite a reputation for our food here. I'm delighted you want to stay with us, Helen."

As Mum beams with pride, I glance at Chantelle, amazed to see the smallest flicker of a smile. "I think you should stay, too," she says quietly.

"Really?" I ask.

She nods as her cheeks burn pink.

"If we do get Promise back," Ryan says, "where will we keep her? I bet moorings cost a fortune in London."

Mum pushes back her hair. "That's something we'll have to figure out."

"There's, um . . . a mooring at the bottom of our garden," Leon says tentatively. "We never use it. Maybe she could stay there."

"But. . ." I say, frowning, "what would your mum say about—"

"Never mind Mum," he says quickly. "She doesn't always get her own way, and I know Dad would love it. He reckons it's a waste, us having our own private mooring with no boat to put on it."

"Well, we'll see," Mum says. Maria and Chantelle are clearing the table now, and to give myself a few moments to mull all of this over, I get up to help.

"So, looks like it's all worked out," Chantelle muses as we carry stacks of bowls through to the kitchen and start to load the dishwasher.

"Yeah, I guess so."

Her black-rimmed eyes look guarded as she glances at me. "I, er ... I really am sorry about leaving you in that restaurant."

I shrug and, even though I'm still pretty mad about it, after today's events it no longer seems like such a big deal. "You planned it all along, didn't you?" I ask her. "That's pretty twisted."

She looks at the ground. "I'll pay you back. Mum and Dad say I've got to. I don't have the money right now but I'll give it to you when I do."

"OK," I say lightly.

As we load in the glasses and cutlery, I can sense her giving me quick glances. "I do think it's amazing, what you did today," she adds.

"Mad, though," I say quietly.

She smiles then – the first proper one I've seen. "Completely crazy," she says. "I'd never have dared. But then, you did have Leon with you. . ."

"Yeah," I say, resisting the urge to add, *But I'd have done it anyway. . .*

She pulls out her shiny pink clip and shakes out her hair. "We were together for a while, did you know that?"

"Uh-huh," I say warily.

"It didn't really mean anything, though."

I look at her, not knowing what to say.

"Anyway," she adds briskly, "if you're definitely staying, we should get Dad to do something about your bedroom – that nasty mustard colour on the walls, I mean. I don't know how you can stand it. Shall I ask him for you?"

"Er . . . that would be great," I reply, suspecting that this is her slightly clumsy way of attempting to make amends. "Not today, though. Not when he's sitting there with that black eye."

She smiles, and I do too. At least she's trying – kind of. We might never be the best of friends, but it's a start.

"Hey, you two." Mum has appeared in the kitchen doorway. "I think everyone has room for dessert. Could you lift that big tin down from the shelf, please, Chantelle?" She grins at me as Chantelle hands it to her. And when Mum takes off the lid to reveal home-made strawberry tarts, I think I might finally be hungry after all.

CHAPTER
Thirty-five

When we broke up for the holidays back in July, I'd imagined the summer stretching ahead in its usual predictable way, like the stretch of river where I grew up. Bella and I had planned picnics at the lake, but beyond that, we hadn't thought about it much. Back then – which seems an age ago now – summer just *was*. It unfolded, and we drifted along, turning browner by the day as we hopped between the boats.

And how different my life is now, with my room painted a beautiful sky blue and Chantelle turning into the kind of girl I might even be friends with – maybe. Whatever happens, the day we collected Promise from the police pound and brought her down the river, past Bella's boat and all our old friends, will be imprinted on my mind for ever.

It took hours and hours. Mum, Ryan, Leon and I all took turns to steer, and I saw parts of the river I'd never imagined as we approached the city. Here, tall buildings crowded the peaceful water, and instead of ducks there were floating takeaway cartons and the odd shopping trolley or rusty bike poking out. The water was murky and it even *smelled* different. Then the riverbanks became greener again as we came into a smarter part of town, finally mooring at the bottom of Leon's garden. His dad, Michael – an excitable man with wiry dark hair who looked delighted as we tied up – says we can keep Promise here for as long as we like.

Naturally, Mum was pretty shocked when I showed her the contents of my tin. In fact, I felt awful as tears spilled down her cheeks. It was just the two of us that day, sitting in my old cabin together – everyone else was helping Michael to knock the bottom of the garden into shape, where he'd let it grow wild. "I'm sorry, Mum," I said. "I should have told you I'd kept all this stuff."

"No," she said, putting an arm around my shoulders, "I just wasn't thinking straight back then – you know, I even thought about getting rid of Promise, too, as she reminded me so much of your dad. Luckily, Maggie and Phil persuaded me not to. They said it wouldn't be fair on you or your brother to uproot you from everything you knew. I hated it, though, those first few months – everywhere I looked, there was something of your dad's. I felt as if I could hardly breathe."

I swallowed hard and held her hand tightly.

"Anyway," she added, "giving away his things wasn't

fair on you or Ryan either. So I'm really pleased we have all of this."

Ryan was amazed, too, when Mum and I showed him the tin's contents in his bedroom back at the flat. Then he produced *his* secret collection – a ratty old brown cardboard box which he'd kept hidden under his bed for years. It was full of old coins, keys and weird things like badges and even a tarnished necklace. "My treasure from my short-lived career as an archaeologist," he laughed, looking at Mum and me. "And you two thought that metal detector was useless – that I never found anything."

"Why didn't you show us?" Mum gasped.

"Living on the boat, I had to keep *something* to myself," he said. "These were my lucky charms." I knew what he meant exactly: that not everything has to be shared. And it looks as if Ryan's treasures were as important to him as Dad's tin is to me.

Mum smiled as the three of us studied the photos of Dad, the newspaper cuttings and his book of the Seven Wonders of the Ancient World. "You two are far better at keeping things safe than I am," she told us. "I'm amazed I still had all the ownership documents for Promise, to tell you the truth."

And now … well, the weeks have flown by, the cooler September days have turned Leon's garden into a treasure trove of gold and copper leaves, and we're due to start our new school tomorrow. Our uniforms are ready, our new school bags bought, our shoes ridiculously shiny. By "we", I mean Ryan and me – and Leon too.

"Dad reckons it's time I got out into the real world," he laughs as the two of us stretch out, with Murphy between us, on a blanket on Promise's deck.

"D'you mind going to school?" I ask.

His smile warms me from the tips of my ears to my toes. "Of course not. You'll be there, won't you? And, compared to trying to control my sisters, I reckon it'll be a relief."

I laugh and look up at the darkening sky. As long as Leon walks me home, we're allowed to stay out late during the holidays. Well, of course Leon is – he's as free as a bird. But Mum knows I'm safe here, and to me, it feels like home. Even our flat above the Stag does now.

There's no summer house any more, though. Leon's dad was right that it was about to collapse, so he took it down amidst howls of protest from the three girls, and Leon moved all his stuff on to Promise. Now the whole of the inside is papered with maps showing all the places we'll go to one day, if we dare.

It's dusk now, and Murphy scampers after me as I go down into the cabin to fetch candles in jars to bring up on to the deck. Then he curls up with Daisy, who looks like she's his new best friend these days.

Leon lights the candles, arranging them in a row along the edge of the boat. It almost feels just like it was before, especially since Mum stripped off Lily-May and painted back her original name. Except for one thing: she's not my boat any more. She's *ours* — mine and Leon's.

We watch the candles flicker until it's properly night-time, then he kisses me under a dark, dark sky that hangs like velvet above us. And when I look up, there are stars — millions of them, twinkling just for us.

I guess they were there all along.

Acknowledgements

Huge thanks to Cathy, Tania, Erin and my lovely friends from the long-ago narrowboat days, especially John B, Tobi, John T, Amanda and Rob. Happy days on the Regent's Canal — the only time I ever had a posh London postcode!

Fiona Foden Q&A

Like Josie, you once lived on a river boat. What was that like?

I was living in London and happened to go on a boat trip down the Thames where I saw clusters of beautiful houseboats. It looked like the perfect way to live. So I managed to buy a scruffy old boat and lived on the canal in Islington, North London, where there was a community of boaters. We all became friends and hung out together. There was an amazing sense of freedom, and it was especially great in the summer when we'd all be lounging on our decks and having parties, with the occasional boat chugging by. I lived on my boat for two years and was heartbroken to leave!

A Kiss, A Dare… is about first love, and how awkward that can be. What made you decide to write about it?

The setting was my starting point — for years, I've

wanted to write a story set on a boat, to try and convey the magical feeling of living on one. And from that, the storyline started to develop in my mind. I soon figured out that I wanted Josie to go in search of her "stolen" boat, and that she would have a boy with her. I love writing about friendships, crushes and falling in love, as they are universal and rarely as simple as we'd like them to be. That's what makes them so fascinating.

What was the first story you ever wrote?

I started drawing cartoon strips when I was about thirteen and sent them to a comic which no longer exists, called *TV Tops*. They started to buy them for £5 a go which seemed like a HUGE amount of cash back then. When I left school at seventeen, I managed to get a job on a teenage magazine called *Jackie* (also long gone, sadly!) as a trainee writer. My various jobs there involved writing features and organizing the fashion pages, but I would also write the odd story for them, if an idea popped into my mind.

What advice would you give young people who want to write?

Feeling self-conscious can really get in the way of good writing, so the best thing is to make it as relaxed and pleasurable as possible. For me, when I was starting out, that meant writing stories in notebooks and not showing them to anyone for ages. That way, I didn't feel pressured. Write as often as you can – every day if possible. Keep all your old stuff – it's encouraging to look back and see how much you've improved. And remember that even your favourite authors started off just like you, scribbling away in notebooks.

What's the hardest thing about writing books?

Just keeping going, really! It's a long process, but you have to keep pushing on and telling the story, rather than spending too much time trying to make it all perfect. I prefer to write the whole book quickly, on my laptop, and then I go back and improve it.

What were your favourite (and least favourite) subjects at school?

I loved art and English. I'm interested in history now, but at school I found it dull and baffling, perhaps because our teacher was terrifying. Physics and chemistry were totally mysterious to me – I didn't click with them at all. Oh, and I was never picked for the netball or hockey teams. Although I enjoy running now, especially with my dog, I was a complete embarrassment when it came to team sports.

If you weren't a writer, what would you be?

From age thirteen I wanted to work on a teenage magazine, which did happen for me. But at the time I thought it was a silly dream, and decided I wanted to illustrate children's books. I applied for art college but didn't get in – and instead of doing sixth year at school, and trying again, I got the magazine job instead. I still enjoy drawing but I'm not very good. My sixteen-year-old son Sam is far better than I could ever hope to be!

Truth or dare?

I'll tell you a truth – or rather, a sort of confession. I once worked on a TV magazine which was filled with interviews with all the TV stars of the day. And, because I lived on my boat, I didn't actually have a TV. I just had to pretend I knew what was going on, and that I was completely in touch with all the programmes when, really, I didn't have a clue...

If you liked this, you'll love...

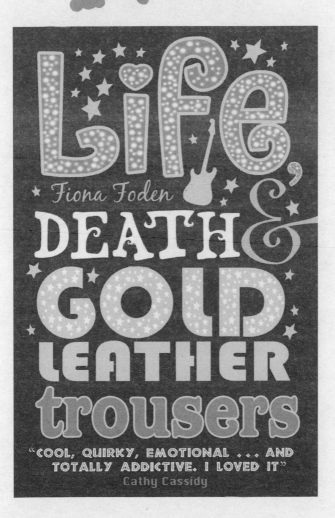

You'll also love...

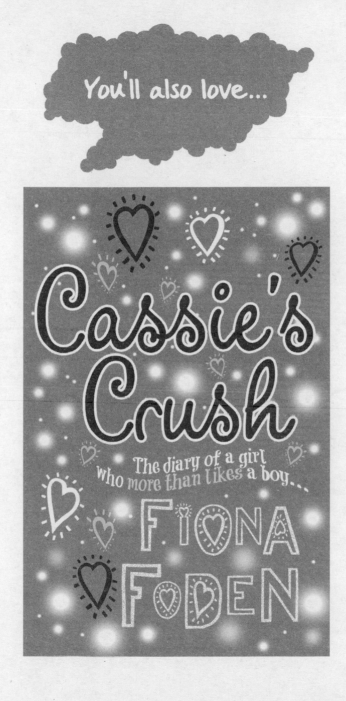

Cassie's Crush

The diary of a girl who more than likes a boy...

FiONA FoDEN